THE HEARTBREAKER

LILI VALENTE

✼ Created with Vellum

To my readers. All my heartfelt thanks.

ABOUT THE BOOK

I've waited years for my drop-dead sexy boss, Tristan Hunter, to notice me as something other than his right-hand gal. But though his dog is deeply in love with me, Tristan and I seem doomed to the friend zone.

Until the night we kiss…

It's all a ruse, of course—our make-out session is for the benefit of the two heartbreakers who dumped us—but very real sparks fly when his lips meet mine.

At least…they're real for me.

* * *

She's my employee, one of my best friends, my dog Luke's not-so-secret crush, and totally off-limits.

So why am I suddenly unable to think of anything but Zoey Childers?

Two days into our fake engagement and I'm dying to take her to bed and show her just how real the heat could be between us. But crossing that line wouldn't just be borderline unethical—it could be lethal to our friendship.

Zoey isn't a casual fling kind of girl, and after the way things ended with my ex, I don't trust my instincts when it comes to love.

I should call off this fake engagement before somebody gets hurt, but how to say "no" to something real with Zoey when every bone in my body is dying to say "yes"?

CHAPTER 1

TRISTAN

*A*fter sixteen months, two weeks, and three days, I'm finally at a place where I can attend a wedding without spending every single second thinking about the one who got away. The one who *threw* me away when she woke up one morning, decided being with one man for the rest of her life was a fate worse than death, dropped my ring on the bedside table, and bolted as fast as her shapely legs could carry her.

Kim.

For a solid month after she left, I wasn't worth shooting in the face. I lost weight, I lost my sense of humor, I damned near lost my will to live.

I know my brothers thought I was being a melodramatic, lovesick bastard, but Kim and I had been together since high school. I had been head over heels in love with the girl she was and the woman she'd become and had my heart set on all the plans we had for our future.

She was my family, every bit as much as my father and my brothers.

More so, if I'm honest.

Kim didn't expect me to be the calm, level-headed voice of reason all the time. Kim let me be a complete person, living in 3D. She saw every side of me—light and dark, serious and silly, dedicated and flexible, determined, and yet still sometimes so lost as to what I should do next.

I thought she was The One. I was fucking positive of it, in fact.

And when The One decides to call off your engagement and move to the other side of the world to live on a continent full of deadly land and sea creatures…

Well, it's enough to give a man a complex.

The Australian beaches have jellyfish with a sting so excruciating the pain alone is enough to *kill* a man. They have ticks whose bites can send people into anaphylactic shock, spiders with venom that causes organ failure, and massive saltwater crocodiles that can clock in at nearly twenty feet long and over two thousand pounds.

Not to mention sharks.

Three kinds.

"She hates sharks. I should have known she'd be back," I mutter over the rim of my beer, fighting the urge to turn and glare at the woman across the room.

Of all the bars in all the world, why did my ex and her new man have to walk into this dive in the middle of my brother's wedding reception? Right when I was

2

proving to myself and all my concerned family members that I was over her and moving the fuck on?

My older brother Deacon grunts in solidarity. "You want to get out of here?" He pushes his half-finished beer away and slides off his stool. "I'm newly retired and have nowhere to be for the first time in my life. We could hit a few bars in Santa Rosa, drink too much, get a car home, eat pancakes at three a.m."

My lips curve. "Normally I'd say yes, but I've got to be at the shelter at seven tomorrow. Someone finally agreed to adopt that domesticated buffalo, but they need to pick him up early before they head home to Mendocino. Then I've got a pair of ferrets who need medicine, and a blind cat who may or may not have diabetes—we're getting her tested. And then Zoey and I have to run numbers and place a food order before noon. Going to be a big day."

Deacon's blue eyes crinkle at the edges as he claps a hand on my shoulder. "Talking to you always makes me glad I have kids instead of pets."

I grimace. "I hear you."

"Call me if you change your mind," he says, backing toward the door. "And whatever you do, don't talk to her. Don't even look at her if you can help it."

I nod and lift a hand, though I have no intention of following my brother's advice. As soon as Kim pulls her giggling, flushed face out of her new boyfriend's asshole, I'm going to wave hello with my most relaxed smile and make it clear that I couldn't care less that she's moved on.

Then, I'll leave. Then, and only then.

I may be "the nice brother," but I still have my pride, dammit.

I take a slow, shallow sip of my beer, determined to nurse it as long as I have to, when Zoey suddenly appears in front of me, wide-eyed and clearly in a panic, blocking my view of Kim and her beefy new man-candy.

"Hide me," she whispers, her face going so pale the freckles dusted across her nose and cheeks stand out in stark relief. "You have to hide me. Please. Just tuck me under your jacket or a bar stool. Something!"

"Why? What's wrong?" I sit up straighter, doing my best to offer her cover. Zoey is my oldest employee, but she's also a good friend. If she needs to hide, I'll help her.

I can't imagine what has her so upset. She's usually the most upbeat, sunny person I know.

"This horrible person I went to college with is here," she says, scooting closer to the bar and my stool. "She made fun of me for years, and now she's here with Bear, my ex-boyfriend, who I thought was the sweetest person in the world. But if he's with her, he's not sweet. He's awful. And she's awful, and I'm afraid if they see me I'm going to cry or faint or throw up in the middle of the dance floor."

"All right, no worries, we've got this." I ease off my stool, my own drama forgotten. "Tell me where they are. I'll be your human shield, block you from view until we get to the door, and then we'll bail. Go get a drink somewhere with no assholes in it."

Her shoulders sag, and her bright blue eyes flood with gratitude. "Thank you, Tristan. So much. They're over by the window. The big guy with the fuzzy face and the girl with the platinum blond hair and a chunk of ice for a heart."

I go still, chest tightening. Surely she can't mean…

I mean, I know Kim isn't the person I thought she was, but surely she wouldn't torture a sweetheart like Zoey? "The woman in the red sweater? Black pants?"

Zoey's forehead furrows as she nods. "Yes. Why?"

"That's Kim," I blurt out.

"Kim." She frowns harder before her brows shoot up in sudden understanding. "*The* Kim? *Your* Kim?"

"Yes," I whisper. "Her picture used to be on my desk in my office."

"Well, I never go into your office," she hisses, looking distressed. "I respect your space. You're my boss."

"She came to the benefit gala with me three years in a row. Surely you met her there. Or when she used to bring me lunch?"

"No, I never saw her, Tristan," Zoey insists. "I never had a date for the gala, and somehow I managed to miss the lunch visits from your evil ex-girlfriend. Believe me, if I'd known you were dating Kimberly Khan, I would have remembered it." She exhales sharply, adding beneath her breath, "And I would have quit my job, so I never had to risk running into her again."

Damn, that sounds serious. "What did she do to you?" I ask, unable to help myself.

"How many hours have you got," she grumbles, glancing over her shoulder before turning back to me with a soft yip of terror. "Oh my God, she's coming! She's coming; she's seen us. What do we do? I rode here with Violet, and I can tell she's not ready to leave." Zoey grabs handfuls of my jacket, clinging to me with a desperation that makes my pulse race.

I look down into her panicked face and am suddenly struck by how pretty she is.

And if there's one thing I know Kim hates, it's competition. For anything—even for things she's decided she doesn't want anymore.

Trusting my gut, I lift a hand, sliding my fingers gently through Zoey's sun-streaked brown hair as I whisper, "Just go with me, okay?"

Her lips part, but before she can speak, I cover her mouth with mine, kissing her slowly, gently at first, shocked by the sizzle that races across my skin in response. Before I know it, her arms are around my neck, and I'm tugging her curvy body against mine, and my tongue is stroking into her sweet mouth while she gives as good as she gets, pressing closer as the kiss grows deeper, hotter.

Soon I'm aching and entertaining all sorts of inappropriate thoughts about my number one employee. Thoughts about Zoey laid out on my bed while I kiss every freckle on her body, while I taste her, tease her, make her bright eyes flash even brighter as I make her come.

I lose all awareness of time, space, or approaching exes until a familiar laugh tinkles through the air.

Zoey and I jump apart, and I turn to see Kim

standing inches away, grinning up at me with an expression that says she isn't buying our act for a minute.

Only...it wasn't an act.

Well, it was when I decided to kiss Zoey. But now...

God, I don't know what that was, only that I want to do it again as soon as possible.

"Hi, Kim," Zoey says in a flat voice. "How are you?"

"I'm great. And how are you, Zoey? Still getting drunk and kissing random men at parties, I see."

"She was kissing her fiancé, actually," I find myself saying, my mouth making executive decisions before my brain can weigh in. I'm dimly aware of Zoey staring up at me with a stunned expression, but I just hug her closer and smile. "You ready to go, babe? Or do you want to grab another beer?"

"I'm r-ready to go, honey," Zoey stammers. "Good to see you, Kim."

"Totally," Kim says, sounding less confident than she did a moment before. "See you two around, then. I'm here until the New Year, when Bear and I are heading back to Swan Valley for the harvest." She laughs and rolls her eyes. "Weirdly enough, we're actually renting a condo behind our old place, Tristan. So, I guess we'll all be neighbors."

Inwardly I curse the cruel and heartless Fates—living next door to my ex will be about as much fun as a standing date for a root canal—but outwardly I simply smile and say, "Guess so. See you around, neighbor."

Zoey and I head for the door, my arm around her

waist, playing the happy couple while I silently wonder what fresh hell my big mouth has gotten me into this time. Me *and* Zoey. Because there's no easy way out of this lie.

The only way to escape with our dignity intact is to pretend to be engaged—at least until Kim and Bear go back to the land Down Under.

I do some quick calculations as I tuck Zoey into the passenger's seat of my truck and circle around to the other side—Halloween is a week away. Then roughly four and a half weeks in November, another four and a half in December…

Ten weeks.

To save face, Zoey and I are going to have to pretend to be madly in love for ten whole weeks.

Fuck…

I slide into the driver's seat and slip the key into the ignition. "I'm so sorry, Zoey. I don't know what I was thinking. I just opened my mouth and craziness came out."

"Just drive," she whispers. "And look happy. She's watching us through the window. We can talk more on the road."

"Gotcha." I force a smile as I reach across the truck to give Zoey's knee an apologetic squeeze, surprised again by the electricity that hums across my skin when we touch. Memories of the way her full lips felt pressed to mine, of the way she tastes—like salted strawberries and summertime—rush through my head as I pull out onto Highway One and aim the truck east, away from the coast. Zoey's been my right-hand woman for three years, and not once in that entire time has our relationship been anything but professional. I was with Kim when I hired her, but even if I'd been single, I'm not the kind of guy who hits on his employees. I would never abuse my position that way or do anything to make my staff feel uncomfortable.

Until now, asshole. Ten minutes in Kim's presence and you're already losing your shit again.

I wince at the thought but refuse to let the voice of doom prove prophetic.

I will figure a way out of this mess with my self-respect, my professional reputation, and my friendship with Zoey intact. All three mean too much to me to settle for anything less.

"I don't know about you, but I could really go for a glass of wine," Zoey says, rubbing the bridge of her nose. "I'm not nearly tipsy enough to unpack the past fifteen minutes."

"Want to hit the Locals on the square? My treat?"

"Sounds good." Zoey sighs as she leans back in her seat, her face pale. She looks tired and more stressed than I've ever seen her, making me wonder all over again what the hell Kim did to her back when they were in school.

But she also looks...beautiful. Ethereal in the moonlight, with her lips softly parted and her perfect profile highlighted against the night sky.

How on earth have I worked next to this woman every day for years and not noticed that her mouth is a work of fucking art? Or that she's every bit as sexy as she is sweet?

Better question—how am I going to go back to being her boss and friend now that I know how incredible it feels to kiss her?

CHAPTER 2

ZOEY

I *kissed* Tristan.

Tristan *kissed* me.

My lips and Tristan's lips have met, my tongue and Tristan's tongue have made each other's intimate acquaintance, and after years of crushing and daydreaming and far too many late-night fantasies, I know exactly what it's like to make out with my boss.

It is…addictively amazing. Euphorically magnificent. Blissfully mind-blowing and utterly and completely perfect in every way.

His kiss was like fresh sea air and something seductively smoky—like a campfire on a cool spring night—and I'm already dying for another taste.

Okay, fine. I want more than a taste.

I want Tristan's body pressed to mine, Tristan's hands pinning my wrists to the mattress, Tristan's mouth hot on my throat as he tells me he's been dying to make love to me since the moment I walked into his animal shelter with a degree in social work and a passion for rescuing Northern California's four-legged friends. I want his lips everywhere, his hands everywhere, and I would gladly sell a piece of my soul to know what it feels like to have nothing between us but skin.

In the past three years, as my temporary break from the dating scene to focus on work slowly became something closer to a vow of celibacy, I thought I'd moved past the roaring hunger for physical connection. Just as I'd outgrown pizza and beer as diet staples, I'd assumed I'd also outgrown the hormones that had made Bear and I the butt of our friends' jokes during our college days. Back then, the thought of going more than a day or two without jumping into bed with my big, furry boyfriend was unthinkable. I was hooked on his body, the closeness we shared, and all the incredible, previously undiscovered things he made me feel.

But now I'm older and wiser. I'm a twenty-six-year-old woman with a demanding full-time job, responsibilities, and the maturity to realize sex isn't that big a deal in the grander scheme of things. Like ice cream, it's a delicious indulgence, but I'm perfectly capable of going without it when I'm watching calories in pre-swimsuit season or focusing my attention on other things.

Or so I'd thought…

Oh, what a fool I've been. What an idiot. What a dangerously dimwitted dumb-dumb, wandering around without a clue that I was a sex-deprived ticking time bomb, ready to explode the moment Tristan Hunter pulled me into his arms and kissed me like there was no one else in the world.

As we make our way into Locals and slide onto stools at the end of the dimly lit bar, where only a few other patrons are passing a lazy, late-October Sunday night, it takes every bit of self-control I possess not to wrap my arms around his neck, push up on tiptoe, and see if our second kiss will be as explosive as our first. This situation absolutely calls for all my usual reserve and caution—this man is my boss, for God's sake—but right now hunger is calling the shots.

I'm starving, famished, and if I'm not careful that wild, ravenous part of me is going to do something so stupid no amount of apologies the morning after will be able to make it better.

I should leave.

Now.

At the very least, I should order coffee or tea—something cozy and caffeinated to help shore up my inhibitions instead of stripping them away.

But when Tristan suggests a Pinot he enjoyed the last time he was here, I let him order two glasses, and when the bartender sits mine in front of me, I grip the heavy glass in both hands and take a healthy gulp. It tastes like dried cherries, peat, and secret, earthy things that only come out at night, and it is absolutely *way* too sexy for drinking with a friend.

Especially considering all my kiss-addled mind can think about is how well Tristan's mouth would pair with this sinfully delicious red…

"So, as far as I see it, we have two choices moving

forward," Tristan says, his dark eyes serious and his brow furrowed, making it clear how much he regrets the past half hour.

I nod, forcing an all-business expression onto my face, even as my heart curls into a sad ball behind my ribs. Yes, I've had a crush on this man for years. And yes, that kiss was light-up-the-night breathtaking...for me. But clearly, Tristan doesn't feel the same way. He's worried about the fallout, not about how right it felt to lock lips with someone he previously considered "just friends" material.

"Option one, we go with the lie and pretend to be engaged until Kim and Bear move back to Australia," he says, making my stomach assume the fetal position along with my heart, my gut instantly recognizing what a bad idea that is.

There's no way I'll be able to pretend to be in love with Tristan for months without giving away my very real feelings for him. From my first week on the job three years ago, when I watched him coax a starving, abused cocker spaniel out of her kennel and into his arms with nothing but his gentle voice and a promise from his heart that he would never let anyone hurt her again, I've been gone on this man. And since that day, he's proven in a thousand different ways that he's worthy of every ounce of my unrequited devotion.

One look at Tristan and any woman can see that he's gorgeous—a face like a Latin pop star with the body of an Olympic athlete and dark, silky, shampoo-commercial-model worthy hair that hangs down into his eyes when he's gone too long without a trim—but it's his heart that's truly one in a million. Tristan is the kindest, most generous, most thoughtful person I've ever met. He's also an incredibly hard worker, devoted to the animals in his care, and not afraid to fight for what he believes in when he and our board of directors clash on what's best for the shelter.

And now I know that he kisses like Ryan Gosling in *The Notebook*—like a man who wouldn't hesitate to carry you up a hill, across the lawn, into the house, up the stairs, and down the hall to the bedroom, kissing you the entire way because he refuses to pull his lips from yours for a single freaking second, even if it means exerting Herculean amounts of strength and will.

I'm so drawn into the fantasy—and imagining what it would be like to kiss Tristan in the rain—that I zone out for a second.

"So...what do you think, Zoey?" Tristan asks in a tone that makes me think it isn't the first time he's asked the question. "Option one or option two?"

I shake my head, laughing as I reach for my wine. "I'm sorry, I spaced. It's been a long day. What was option two again?"

"Option two is we lay low and hope the engagement doesn't come up. But if we happen to run into Kim or Bear, and they happen to ask about it, then we say that you called it off." He shrugs. "Say you got cold feet or something, whatever you think is best. As long as it makes it look like I'm the loser and you're happily moving on with your life."

I frown, hating that idea. "I don't want to make you look like a loser."

"But I deserve it." He holds my gaze with an intensity that makes my thin blue sweater and gauzy chiffon skirt suddenly feel too warm. "I'm the one who got us into this mess."

"That's not true. I came to you, begging for your help. And you helped. You did." I take another sip of my wine, hoping it will hide the flush I can feel heating my cheeks.

"Did I really?" he asks, arching a brow.

"Well, Kim didn't get away with making me feel two feet tall," I say. "And Bear doesn't think I'm a pathetic loser who's been mourning our breakup for the past three years, so... Things could definitely have been worse."

Tristan studies me for a long moment, until I have to fight the urge to squirm.

"What?" I ask, swiping a finger self-consciously across the edges of my lips, wondering if I have a red wine mustache.

He shakes his head. "Nothing, I just... Have you really been mourning him for three years? Is that why you don't date much?"

No, I've been dreaming about you, boss man. Crushing on you. Fantasizing about what it would be like to be the lucky woman you come home to every night.

Thankfully, instead of any of those mortifying confessions, I say in my best all-business voice, "Not at all. I loved Bear, and we had a few great years together, but we weren't compatible long term. I think we both knew that, even though he was the one who officially decided to end it."

"Why weren't you compatible?" Tristan asks. "I mean, if that's not too personal…"

"No, it's not too personal. I just…" I swirl my wine, watching the ruby liquid change colors as it flows around the edge of the glass. "I always saw myself settling down and putting down roots after college, and Bear wanted to travel, roaming the world until he found a place to stick for a while and then moving on when that gig wasn't fun anymore. That kind of life wasn't for me. I like community and a sense of place. I like feeling like—"

"Like you belong." Tristan finishes my thought with a nod. "I get it. I'm the same way. That's why I never left Sonoma County, even when Kim transferred to Sacramento instead of staying at Sonoma State with me. We'd been together for two years at that point, but it was easier to do the long-distance thing with my girlfriend than to leave everyone here behind." He rolls his eyes. "But you know my family. There's always some kind of drama in the works."

"I love your family," I say sincerely. "They're great. I can see why you wanted to stay close to them."

"But if I'd gone with Kim, I might have seen through her so much sooner." Tristan leans in closer, making my pulse pick up. "What did she do to you, Zoey? I've never seen you upset like that."

"Oh, just…kid stuff really." I shake my head, swallowing hard as I realize how little I can tell Tristan about the great and evil Khan. He almost married Kim, for God's sake, and he was completely devastated when she broke it off.

If he finds out the entire ugly truth, he'll feel like even more of a fool, and I refuse to do that to him.

"Really?" Tristan arches a dubious brow. "Didn't seem like kid stuff to me."

"It's old news. Seriously, nothing worth rehashing," I insist, pushing on when his expression remains skeptical. "I was overreacting, which means this is as much my fault as yours. So…" I pull in a deep breath, ignore the voice screaming in my head that this is the worst idea ever, bar none, and smile. "So, let's do it. Let's pretend to be engaged until they leave."

"You're sure? Because I don't mind looking like an idiot. It wouldn't be the first time, and I'm sure it won't be the last."

"No way," I say, forcing certainty into my tone. "Neither one of us is playing the fool this time. We'll pretend to be engaged, make sure Kim and Bear see that we're deliriously happy without them, and send them back to Australia knowing that we're over them and moving on."

His shoulders relax and some of the tension fades from around his eyes. "Sounds good," he says, before adding with a laugh, "I mean, it doesn't sound good, it sounds crazy, and I'm sorry I got us into this mess. But making sure Kim knows I'm not sitting in a corner, rocking naked in a puddle of my own tears, mourning the end of us, will be nice."

"Rocking naked in your own tears isn't pretty," I agree, though I honestly doubt Tristan could be anything but ridiculously beautiful naked, no matter what else he was doing at the time.

And that's the kind of thing I have to *stop* thinking if I'm going to have any shot at pulling this off.

"No, it isn't." He rubs a hand across his jaw, making a soft scratching sound as his skin brushes stubble, making my lightly whisker-burned lips tingle.

I have whisker burn from kissing him, and right now all I want to do is kiss him again. Instead, I take a drink of my wine—a big drink, draining it all the way to the bottom—and set my glass down with a firm nod.

"Then it's settled." I slip off my stool and grab my purse from the hook beneath the bar. "We'll start tomorrow. See you at work."

"Oh, okay." Tristan blinks and reaches for his suit coat on the stool next to him. "Just let me pay the bill and I'll drive you home."

I wave a breezy hand through the air and back toward the door. "No worries, I'll call a car. No reason for you to drive all the way out to Dry Creek again."

"But I—"

"Seriously, I'm good. No worries," I insist, head swimming from the combined influence of the wine and Tristan standing there looking like sex on a stick in gray suit pants, a crisp white button-down, and the deep-charcoal and gold vest all of the groomsmen wore for his brother's wedding.

I spent all afternoon at an uber-romantic wedding, the evening sipping champagne at a reception packed with people who are madly in love, and ended the night with an earth-shattering kiss before getting fake engaged to my real-life crush. It's been an over-the-top swoony kind of day. That's the only reason I'm finding it so hard to keep from running to Tristan, driving my fingers through his hair, and pulling his mouth to mine.

I just need to get some distance and some sleep, and by tomorrow morning I'll be back in my right mind.

So even though Tristan clearly thinks I'm insane, I wave cheerily, say, "See you tomorrow," and make a run for it.

I find a cab waiting not far from the bus stop in Healdsburg's historic town square, slide into the back seat, and give the driver the address of the animal shelter. In fifteen minutes, I'll be back in my cozy little apartment above the storage room, tucked in with a good book and a cup of insanity-reducing chamomile tea.

And when I wake up tomorrow, it will be a new day, shiny and fresh with no head-spinning romance in it.

"Except for the part where you and Tristan are going to be pretending to be in love for several months," I mutter, not caring if the driver thinks I'm crazy.

I probably am, but nuts or not, there's no turning back now.

CHAPTER 3

From the texts of Tristan Hunter
and Deacon Hunter

Deacon: Just checking to make sure you got home safe,
sound, and with no Kim-Kahn-induced battle scars. Tap
me back when you get the chance.

Tristan: I'm home. The safe and sound part is debatable.

Deacon: Shit. You talked to her, didn't you? After I
warned you not to. What happened to listening to
words of wisdom from your oldest brother?

Tristan: I listened. She's the one who came over to talk
to me.
Right after Zoey begged me to hide her from her ex-
boyfriend, who turned out to be Kim's new boyfriend.

Deacon: No shit?

Tristan: No shit. And then one thing led to another, and I ended up making out with Zoey at the bar and telling Kim that Zoey and I were engaged.

Deacon: Oh fuck.

Tristan: Yeah, that pretty much sums it up. So now Zoey and I are fake engaged until after the New Year, when Kim and her new guy head back to Australia.

Deacon: You realize that's insane, right?

Tristan: Oh yeah. Completely insane. I offered to let Zoey fake dump me, so at least she could save face, but she didn't want to go that route. So, I guess I need to swing into Jillian's on the Square before work tomorrow and get her a ring.

Deacon: And somehow you've got Dad and the rest of them convinced that you're the sanest man in the family. That's a solid con you've got going on there, Tris.

Tristan: Pride makes a madman of the best of us. I just hope Zoey and I can get through this with our friendship intact.

Deacon: Yeah, she's a sweet girl.

Tristan: And incredible at her job and amazing with animals and people and a complete professional in every way. I don't know what I'd do without her.

Deacon: So does this mean the kiss was awful?
Or that the kiss was so good you're reminding yourself why you can't have a fling with the person you depend on to keep your work life running smoothly?

Tristan: Door number two...

Deacon: Oh man, you really are in trouble.

Tristan: Tell me about it.
I've been sitting here for an hour, staring at my phone, trying to convince myself to text her and call the whole thing off.

Deacon: But you can't. Because you want an excuse to kiss her again.

Tristan: Because I want to prove to Kim that I'm not the pathetic wreck of a person she dumped on his ass a year and a half ago. That's what this is about, Deacon. Zoey and I are just friends and coworkers—that's all we've ever been, and that's all we're ever going to be.

Deacon: Why? She's beautiful, sweet, hard-working, apparently a dynamite kisser.
You got something against freckles or something?

Tristan: No, I don't have a thing against freckles.
I like freckles, especially on her…
But it's not going to happen. It can't.
Even if Zoey were interested in me in that way—which
she's not—we work together. I don't want to get into a
relationship with someone who depends on me for her
paycheck. That's creepy, and I don't want to be a creep.

Deacon: But a fake engagement with your subordinate
is A-Okay.

Tristan: Fine. Point taken. I'll text her and call it off.

Deacon: Sure you will…

Tristan: I've really missed your smug side, you know?
I'm so glad you're retired and are going to be around all
the time, making sure none of us have to do without
big-brotherly condescension in our lives ever again.

Deacon: I'm not smug, buddy. I've just been there.
Chemistry is like toothpaste—once it's out of the tube,
it's not going back in. Fake relationship, real relationship, or strained relationship because you're trying to
slap a friendly label on something that's not just-
friendly anymore… One way or another, you and Zoey
are going to have to deal with the consequences of
learning that you like to kiss each other.

Tristan: You're assuming she feels the same way, but she

doesn't. As soon as we decided on a game plan, she couldn't get away from me fast enough.

Deacon: All right. Maybe I'm wrong. Maybe you're a shit kisser and she can't wait to go back to being platonic coworkers as soon as the nightmarish experience of being your fake true love is over.

Tristan: Thanks. I feel so much better.

Deacon: You're welcome. Feel free to text any time. The twins are away at college, and until I decide what's next work-wise, I've got nothing but free time. And don't worry—I won't share your big news with Dad or any of the other gossipmongers around here. Your secret is safe with me.

Tristan: Thanks.

Deacon: You're welcome.
Oh, and make sure to get her something special for the ring, just in case.

Tristan: Now who's crazy?

Deacon: I am. But I'm also right more often than people like to give me credit for. Especially the people I helped raise into almost grown people. The twins are both refusing to put part of their paycheck into the retirement plans I've started for them. They think they're too young to think about retirement. But you're never too young to think about retirement.

Tristan: I hear you, brother, but I'm not a college kid who wants to spend my money on gas, beer, and taking my girlfriend to Six Flags every other weekend.

Deacon: Rollercoasters. Jesus. What a waste. It causes me physical pain to see them flushing their hard-earned money away like that.
But...at least they're happy.

Tristan: And doing great in school and in their relationships and still coming home to visit their obnoxious family once a month. I call that winning big. You've got two great boys, and they're going to keep growing into great men. No doubt in my mind.

Deacon: And there's no doubt in mine that you're going to find someone a hundred times better than Kim. Maybe very, very soon...

Tristan: You're listening skills are for shit, but thanks. Love you, man. Glad you're home for good.

Deacon: Me, too, brother. Me, too.

CHAPTER 4

*G*et her something special for the ring...just in case...

Deacon's words float around in my brain all night, taunting me in a sing-song voice, making sleep hard to come by.

He's a good man, my brother, but he's also out of his damned mind. I was engaged once before, and the woman I thought was going to be my forever dumped me because she couldn't imagine being with *just one guy* for the rest of her life.

A rousing endorsement of my irresistibility to the opposite sex, it was not.

And even if Zoey and I ended up being as good a fit romantically as we are professionally, I'm not sure where I stand on long-term love anymore.

Sure, I used to be a shameless romantic, a smug, happily-coupled person who thought he had love all figured out. But I clearly didn't know my ass from a hole in the ground. The woman I thought was my perfect match turned out to be a heart-breaking asshole.

And a bully, to boot, judging by Zoey's meltdown last night.

I'm not buying the "kid stuff" excuse for a second. Zoey isn't the kind to beg to be hidden from someone because they had a falling out about who was going to be president of the debate team. No, I'm guessing Zoey softened the story to spare me sordid tales of my ex's shitty behavior. That's exactly what I would expect from a sweetheart like her, and yet another reason it would be a bad idea for us to be anything but friends.

I don't like hurting people—anyone, ever, if I can help it—but it would be especially miserable to hurt someone like Zoey.

The woman doesn't have a mean bone in her body or much in the way of an emotional support system. Her dad ran off when she was a kid, her mom died when she was a freshman in college, and she doesn't have any other family in the picture as far as I can tell. Yes, she has good friends, but she spends most of her life at the shelter—either working or at her on-site apartment, serving as our go-to in case of animal-related emergencies. If she and I started dating and it ended badly, it would be like Daryl the Doberman with the bad bladder took a piss all over her life.

And I don't want Zoey's life to be pissed on.

Especially not because of something I've done.

"This is a bad idea, Luke," I mutter as I pull into my parking space in front of the shelter and shut off the engine. But beside me, my eternally optimistic golden retriever is as blissed out as he always is to be arriving at work, where he knows he'll have at least nine quality hours with the object of his undying affection.

Luke's been in love with Zoey since we rescued him and his littermates from a puppy farm two years ago. He lives to lie at her feet, gobble the treats she keeps in a jar on her desk, and break into her apartment while Zoey and I are busy elsewhere and eat her socks.

And occasionally, her panties, when he can find a pair lying around...

On our last emergency trip to the vet, Luke vomited up a skimpy pink lace thong on the waiting room floor while we were waiting for an exam room, making Zoey blush so red I wasn't sure her cheeks would ever return to their normal color.

At the time, I'd simply been mortified by my dog's bad behavior and how deeply it had embarrassed her. Now, I can't help thinking about what Zoey would look like in a pair of skimpy lace panties and nothing else...

My stupid brother was right.

The toothpaste is out of the tube, and it's *not* going back in.

I'm having all kind of never-before-entertained thoughts about Zoey, and when I see her sitting at her desk—wearing a pair of jeans and a snug long-sleeved tee that molds so tightly to her chest I have to rip my gaze away from her curves—my heart stutters and my palms start to sweat. And then she looks up and smiles, and suddenly all I want to do is kiss her—to pull her into my office, shut the door, and have my way with her on my desk.

Or on the floor...

Or up against the—

"No, bad dog," I shout as Luke jumps into her lap, reverting to a puppy habit we thought we'd broken him of months ago and nearly knocking Zoey's chair over in the process. "Get down, Luke. You don't weigh twelve pounds anymore, man. You're going to crush her." I grab Luke by the collar and guide him back down to the floor. "Sorry about that."

Zoey laughs. "It's fine. At least I know someone's always happy to see me."

I pause, weirdly nervous. I thought I'd talked myself away from the ledge over breakfast this morning and was ready to make the best of a sticky situation. But as my gaze meets hers, my mind goes blank and my sweaty palms begin to itch.

"I mean, I know you're happy to see me, too," Zoey says with another laugh and a shake of her head, making her ponytail swish.

God, she's cute in a ponytail. Dangerously cute...

"I just meant..." Her breath rushes out as she motions toward me. "You know, after last night... I just don't want things to be awkward."

"They aren't, and they won't be," I lie, the jewelry box in my pocket suddenly feeling like an embarrassing growth digging into my ass. "But if you've changed your mind, that's fine. I totally get it. We don't have to go through with it."

"No, no, I'm still in," she says, rubbing Luke's head as he pants appreciatively. "I'm just not sure how one goes about being engaged, you know? I've never been engaged. The closest I got was when my high school boyfriend gave me his class ring before spring break and then wanted it back again a week later because he'd accidentally slept with someone while he was in Cancun."

I arch a brow. "Accidentally?"

Zoey nods as she scratches Luke behind the ears. "Yeah, apparently it's a thing that happens in Cancun. You're walking around, innocently drinking a beer, and all of a sudden you trip in the sand and your penis falls into a stranger's vagina."

I snort in surprise—I've never heard Zoey use the word "penis" or "vagina" before this morning—and she blushes bright pink.

"Sorry," she says. "I'm nervous. My mouth does weird things when I'm nervous."

"Don't be nervous. And your mouth is fine," I say, blood pumping faster as I remember how good her mouth felt pressed to mine. "It's perfect."

Jesus. Shut the fuck up, Tristan! Stop talking about her mouth. Stop looking at her mouth and pull your shit together, man.

Clearing my throat, I reach into my pocket and pull out the jewelry box. "And I can help you with the engaged learning curve. First thing on the agenda, of course, is the ring."

Zoey's eyes go wide as I open the case. "Oh my God, Tristan. It's beautiful. Like something from a fairy tale."

"It was my grandmother's," I say, ridiculously pleased that she likes it. I've always thought the vine-and-flower detailing around the stone was something special, but

Kim had said the rose gold setting was "tacky" and the diamond too small for a modern bride. "I was going to pick something up at the jewelry store, but then I remembered this and thought it would be perfect. Classy, but fun. Like you."

Zoey blinks faster, looking flustered. "Well, crap. If I'd known you thought I was classy, I wouldn't have made Cancun penis jokes. Now I've ruined the illusion."

"I like your jokes," I say, holding up the box. "Try it on, let's see if it fits."

She reaches for the ring, only to pull her hands back to her chest with a shake of her head. "No, I can't, Tristan. What if it slips off and I lose it in the bulk cat food? Or I break or bend it while I'm cleaning cages or something? I'll never forgive myself."

"It's not going to bend or break. And if it's too big, we'll get it sized." Plucking the ring from the stiff velvet, I reach for her hand. The moment my fingers brush hers, electricity pulses across my skin, assuring me the chemistry from last night is still in full effect. I look up, catching her gaze and holding it as I slide the ring onto her slim finger. "Just like I thought," I say, "a perfect fit."

Zoey's blue eyes glitter and her lips part, but she doesn't speak. She steps closer, until the spring rain and strawberry smell of her fills my head. She smells so fucking good I want to bury my face in her neck and inhale her, memorize the exact notes that make up Eau de Zoey, then kiss my way up her throat to claim her pretty mouth.

I'm half a heartbeat away from giving in—from kissing her while stone-cold sober and proving this is way more complicated than a little pretend between friends—when Luke barks. A second later, one of his paws lands on my shoulder, the other on Zoey's, and he shoves his grinning face between ours with an excited whimper.

"Hey, buddy," Zoey says, laughing. "You like the ring, too?"

Luke responds by licking Zoey's cheek—shamelessly kiss-blocking the man who feeds him. But this time, I owe him one. Kissing Zoey isn't on my agenda, at least not in private, purely for pleasure.

I've been saved by dog slobber in the nick of time. Now to get to my office, get myself under control, and establish some ground rules before this goes any further.

"Aw, thanks, big guy, I love your kisses." Zoey scratches Luke's ears before lifting his paws off our shoulders. "But you know better than to jump up. Now go lie down on your bed. Go, or we're going to have to take you back to obedience class. Again."

With a tucked tail and a shamed look in his melted-chocolate eyes, Luke trots over to the bed in the corner of the office and curls up with his head mournfully propped on his paws.

Zoey clucks her tongue. "Such a sad face. I would feel sorry for him if he weren't an absolute rascal."

"He really is," I say with a smile. "He's not stupid. He just has zero interest in following the rules."

"Reminds me of your brother." Zoey snaps her fingers as she turns back to me. "Which reminds me—I feel terrible about leaving the reception last night without telling Carrie and Rafe goodbye and thanking them for including me in their special day."

"Don't worry about it. They won't care. They're not stand-on-ceremony people."

"I know, but I still feel bad. I like to remember my manners and prove I wasn't raised by wolves." She glances down at the ring as she lifts her hand, making the stone catch the light and flare like a tiny star. "Are you absolutely sure you want me to wear this? It's a family heirloom, Tristan. Even if it isn't important to you, your brother or your mom might want it, right?"

"Who said it isn't important to me?" I brush a loose curl behind her ear, unable to keep my fingers from lingering on the soft, warm skin of her neck. "And I trust you with my family heirloom. Completely."

She looks up, and I swear I can feel her pulse beat faster, throbbing softly beneath my fingertips. "I... I don't know what to say." Her breath rushes out. "And that doesn't happen to me, Tristan. I always have something to say. This fake engagement is already making me weird, and it's just the two of us alone in the office. What am I going to do when we're in front of other people?"

Before I can assure her it's going to be fine, she rushes on.

"And what about Violet?" She darts a panicked look over my shoulder toward the entrance. "She'll be here any minute! What are we going to tell her? I can't lie to her. Not only would it make me feel terrible, but she would see through me in a freaking heartbeat. She's raised three

CHAPTER 5

*H*olding hands.

Some light cheek kissing.

Maybe a walk through the square arm-in-arm if things are going well and Tristan and I feel ready to take our coupledom for a test run—I've totally got this.

Sure, it's been a while since I've been in a relationship, but it's not like I'm a complete newbie to the world of romance. I've been part of a couple. I've done all of these things before, and at the time they came quite naturally.

But you weren't pretending back then.

*And you didn't do those things while trying to walk the line between being convincing, but not **too** convincing, lest your boss realize there's nothing pretend about how much you want to jump his bones.*

I pause, knuckles hovering above Tristan's door, seriously debating running back to my car and calling in sick to Couple Practice, when it swings open and Tristan appears in the doorway. "Hey. You made it."

"I did," I say, unable to think of anything more clever as I drink in the sight of Tristan fresh from the shower. His dark hair is still damp, and his long-sleeved gray tee clings lightly to his chest. A pair of well-worn jeans complete the casual look, but the way my heart responds to the sight of him is anything but casual.

My pulse picks up, beating faster as I imagine what it would be like to lean in and kiss away the drop of water beaded on his neck, to let my hands slip beneath his shirt and discover the firm muscles beneath. I've seen Tristan without a shirt on exactly twice—once at a beach party fundraiser for the shelter and once while he was mucking out the horse stalls during a heat wave—and both instances are tattooed into my memory bank for all eternity.

Magnificent isn't too strong a word.

Neither is glorious, resplendent, or jaw-dropping.

Just thinking about how beautiful he is half-naked is enough to make me blush. But thankfully, Tristan doesn't seem to notice that I've gone awkwardly mute—or if he does, he's too nice to let on—and motions for me to come in.

"I just stuck dinner in the oven." He leads the way through a small, but cozy, living room furnished in bright blues and white and muted grays, and into the kitchen. "Hope you like roasted root vegetable lasagna."

"Love it," I say as he fetches two bottles of water from the fridge, doing my best not to fidget or do anything else to betray how nervous I am. I was hoping

Luke would help break the ice, but he's nowhere to be seen. "Where's the rascal?"

"He's in his kennel downstairs, watching the U.S. Open for the tenth time."

I grin. "Well, then, he should be a happy boy. He loves his tennis."

"He does. I figured that was the only way to keep him out of our hair. If Luke had his way, there would be no hand-holding without a paw also involved." Tristan nods over his shoulder, a crooked grin curving his lips. "I thought we could hang out in the sunroom. It's nice this time of day."

"Sounds good." I follow him down a hallway, past a closed door, a bathroom, a study, and the open door to his bedroom, where a king-size bed draped in a luxurious-looking, creamy white comforter dominates the space.

The sight of it makes me blush again—because apparently I am thirteen again—and I silently warn my face to get it together. If I keep blushing like a schoolgirl, Tristan is going to realize this is more than a case of fake-relationship jitters.

I step into the sunroom, a gorgeous open space with glass on three sides and all of the windows open wide to let in the autumn breeze. There's a comfy-looking brown couch, two over-stuffed white armchairs, a wide wooden coffee table covered in magazines, and enough potted plants to make it feel like we're settling in for happy hour in the jungle.

Except we're drinking water, of course...

I know that's for the best—I have to learn to be

comfortable without the inhibition-lowering effects of alcohol—but I can't help wishing for a glass of wine. Or a shot of whiskey. Or maybe a blow to the head—anything to quiet the panicky voices chattering away in my skull.

I'm about to confess that I'm still a nervous wreck and beg Tristan to pour me a shot of something to take the edge off, when he plucks a remote from the table, clicks a button, and the first sultry chords of one of my favorite songs twangs from the speakers.

"Crimson and Clover?" I ask, smiling as Tristan turns back to me.

"I know you're a Joan Jett fan." He holds out a hand as Joan moans "ahhhh" over the pulsing guitar, making my throat go tight. "And what better way to get in the couple groove than a slow dance?" He curls his fingers, beckoning me closer. "Come here, Childers. Dance with me."

Pulse pounding and every nerve ending in my body humming in a mixture of terror and anticipation, I slide my hand into his as his arm wraps around my waist. Immediately, he takes control, spinning me in a half circle as he moves away from the coffee table and into the open area near the door to the backyard. I cling to his shoulder, holding on as we sway slowly back and forth.

I've done my share of slow dancing at college parties and fundraisers for Sonoma County charities affiliated with the shelter, but I've never danced like this. Tristan doesn't shuffle side to side, leaving respectable distance for the Holy Spirit the way we did in middle school. He urges me close, molding our bodies together, making me keenly aware of every place we touch.

His muscled chest against my breasts, his firm thighs shifting against mine, his warm hand at the small of my back—it's all so much more intimate than holding hands or his lips brushing my cheek.

It's...overwhelming, so much so that I have no choice but to give in and let him lead, let him spin me left, then right. Let him urge me closer as his palm slides up my back to mold to my ribs, pressing my chest even tighter to his.

My breath rushes out as I sneak a peek at him through my lashes to find him watching me with an inscrutable expression.

"What?" I ask, lips tingling as I realize how close his mouth is to mine.

"Nothing," he murmurs. "You're a good dancer."

"No, *you're* a good dancer," I correct. "I'm a good follower."

"That's a skill all on its own," he says, his fingertips pressing lightly into my back, sending sparks of awareness skittering up and down my spine. "So how is this? Okay?"

I nod loosely, beginning to feel as tipsy as I did last night. Except this time, I'm drunk on Tristan's touch, Tristan's scent, Tristan's body shifting against mine, making me feel like I'm going to die if I don't get another shot of him.

And another.

And another...

"So, you're ready to take practice to the next level?"

he asks as "Crimson and Clover" ends and the sweet, sultry notes of Etta James' "At Last" fill the air.

I nod again, tilting my head back, silently asking for what I want, what I need.

I can't help myself. I *need* to feel his lips on mine, need to know if last night was a freak occurrence or if kissing him will always feel like fireworks exploding in my chest, like lightning streaking through my head, and a four-alarm fire burning beneath my skin, all at once.

Tristan leans closer, closer, until the warmth of him heats my mouth, but he's still not close enough. "Can I kiss you, Zoey?" he finally asks, his voice husky.

I answer him with a soft moan as I press up on tiptoe. The moment our lips connect, the fireworks display ignites behind my closed eyes, even bigger and brighter than the night before. Because this time we're alone, with nothing to distract me from the feel of Tristan's arms holding me close, the taste of him filling my mouth as his tongue parts my lips. Nothing to impede my awareness of Tristan's heart beating in time with mine—faster, harder—as the kiss grows deeper and his hands smooth down my back to cup my bottom through my jeans.

I arch into him, needing to get even closer, gasping against his lips as my belly comes into contact with where he's hard.

Oh my God...

I almost can't believe it, but it's true. Tristan is hard and thick behind the fly of his jeans...because of *me*. Because he *really* wants me—not because we're pretending to be attracted to each other.

I'm still soaring from the realization when suddenly all the heat and sizzle is ripped away, leaving me gasping again—this time from a sudden rush of cold air.

"I'm so sorry." Tristan's gaze drops to the floor as he rakes a hand through his hair. "I don't know what happened. I mean, I know, I just..." He exhales sharply. "I guess some parts of me don't understand the difference between pretend and not pretend. I apologize. Deeply."

"It's okay." I shift uncomfortably from one foot to the other, fingers tangling together to keep myself from reaching for him. "Really, I understand. It's not a big deal."

"I'm your boss, Zoey," he says, his voice rough. "This entire situation is borderline inappropriate to begin with, but I thought I could walk the line... Keep it at least *mostly* professional."

I pull in a breath, on the verge of admitting that he's not the only one feeling unprofessional things. But before I can make any unwise confessions, a familiar voice booms my name. "Zoey?"

I frown, Tristan frowns harder, and we both turn slowly to look out the back window. I catch a glimpse of a furry face partially hidden beneath the limbs of an overloaded orange tree before the voice comes again, "Hey, Zoey! That *is* you!"

"Bear?" I ask, skin crawling despite the friendly smile on my ex-boyfriend's face. Yes, Bear is one of the nicest people I know, but even a nice guy peeping through your back window is a little skeevy. "What are you doing?"

"I'm picking oranges. You guys want some?" He leans over the fence, holding out an enormous fruit that nearly overflows his large hand. "Sorry about interrupting. I was about to crawl back down the ladder, but then I saw your face, Zoey, and..." His cheeks flush above his thick brown beard. "This is weird, right? I'm sorry. It's just been so long since I've seen you, and it was such a nice surprise that I got excited and wanted to say hi. But, dudes, I sincerely apologize for interrupting."

"No, it's fine, Bear," I lie. "I'll be out to say hi in just a second." I turn back to Tristan, adding for his ears only, "Am I crazy, or does it seem like he had no idea he might see me around the neighborhood? Let alone that you and I are allegedly engaged?"

Tristan nods, casting a quick glance over my shoulder at Bear. "You're not crazy. But why would Kim keep that a secret from her live-in boyfriend? Especially considering that you and Bear used to be together?"

I chew my lip as I shrug. "I have no idea, but Kim's choices rarely make any sense to me. Like dumping you," I add as I move toward the door leading into the backyard. "I mean, what woman in her right mind does something like that?"

His dark eyes flash, and the hint of a smile curves his lips. "Thanks. I'm going to go check on the lasagna. Tell Bear hi for me, but be sure to pass on the orange. That tree stopped giving good fruit years ago."

"Will do." I give Tristan a thumbs-up and head out into the yard, heart dancing behind my ribs despite the fact that I'm about to chat with my ex for the first time since he dumped me three years ago. But there was something in Tristan's eyes just then, something that makes me feel…hopeful.

"Wow, Zoey, you look great," Bear says as I approach, his friendly face lighting up with another guileless grin. "How have you been? What have you been up to, woman? It's so great to see you looking so happy and awesome."

"Thanks, Bear. You, too," I say with a smile, no doubt in my mind that's he's being sincere. I don't know what spell Kim has cast over him, but one look into his warm brown eyes is all it takes to convince me he's the same lovable teddy bear of a person he's always been.

We chat for a few minutes about work—mine at the shelter and his as an adventure travel writer who jet sets all over the world—and I'm about to excuse myself when Bear's eyes widen and he points to my left hand. "Oh, wow! So it's serious, then? You and the dude. I mean, you guys are obviously serious, I could tell that even from this side of the fence, but engaged…" His brows creep higher on his forehead. "That's a big step."

"It is." I nod slowly even as my thoughts begin to race.

So Kim definitely *didn't* tell him about Tristan and me. Strange… But it's too late to back away from the pretense now.

"It is absolutely a big step," I continue. "But Tristan's a wonderful guy. The whole package. I'm a lucky girl."

"Nah, he's a lucky guy. You're the whole package and a bag of chips, Zo," Bear says, reminding me why I loved him.

He might not be the most sophisticated or complex

person, but he's kind to a fault, and he never shies away from making another human being feel good about themselves. Even if that human being is his ex-girlfriend. It makes me sick to my stomach to think of him with Kim, but I know better than to try to change a man's mind about the woman in his life. And Bear knows the way Kim treated me, so it's not like he's going in blind.

The warm feeling in my chest cools.

Yes, Bear is a good guy, but he's dating a woman who used to call me a "Food Stamp Tramp" because I was so poor and who spread rumors about me giving frat boys blowjobs in exchange for beer. And all of this because I accidentally caught her doing it in the shower with two guys the first week of our sophomore year. If only I hadn't eaten bad sushi and been forced to race to the dorm bathroom at three a.m., my entire college experience might have been blissfully bully free.

I might never have learned that Kim was cheating on her long-distance boyfriend and she wouldn't have decided I needed to be stomped on like a bug and ground into the dirt for good measure.

Of course, I had no idea at the time that the boyfriend in question was Tristan...

"Well, thanks, Bear. It was good to catch up," I say, backing across the grass. "See you around the neighborhood."

"See you around," he says, adding in a softer voice before I can turn around, "And Zo... Just FYI, Kim is here, too. At the condo. With me. We're kind of...living together. Because we're kind of...together now."

I nod, keeping my expression neutral. "Okay."

"We ran into each other at these Australian caves I was exploring for a blogging gig," he says, clearly feeling guilty about his choice of paramour. "It was wild, bumping into someone from college all the way on the other side of the world, so we went out for beers to catch up. Her dad was sick, and she was pretty bummed, so we made a date for dinner the next night to talk more about family stuff and things just kind of…happened."

"It's fine. Honestly, I don't care. I just…" I hesitate, but can't help but add, "I hope it works out. I hope she treats you the way you deserve to be treated."

"She's changed," Bear says, his eyes all heart and faith. "She truly, honestly has. If she hadn't, I wouldn't be with her. You know that. You know me."

I force a tight smile. "Then best of luck, Bear. Enjoy the oranges."

I hurry across the lawn and let myself into the house without looking back. Yes, I used to know Bear, or at least I thought I did. But it's been four years since we were joined at the hip, and three since we gave up on the long-distance relationship and finally called it quits. He could be a different person now.

So could, Kim, I suppose, though, looking into her eyes last night, she certainly didn't seem any different. She still has that bright, hard…sharpness about her.

Kim is like a cursed diamond or a samurai sword—shiny and beautiful to look at, but sooner or later you're going to regret reaching out to touch her. Tristan certainly did. He was a wreck for months after she left him.

Though, looking at him now, standing over a pan of delicious-smelling roasted veggie lasagna, humming something sexy-sounding beneath his breath as he cuts two large slices, he doesn't seem any worse for wear. In fact, he looks happy. Maybe even really happy. And when he glances up at me, there's a huge smile on his face, "I've figured out a solution to our problem."

"What's that?" I ask, unable to keep from beaming back at him. A Tristan smile turned up to full wattage is my Kryptonite. I'm completely helpless against it.

He's still grinning that thousand-watt grin as he points the lasagna-cutting knife at me and says, "You're fired. Effective immediately."

CHAPTER 6

From the texts of Violet Boden
and Zoey Childers

Zoey: Hey Violet, would you mind staying late on Wednesday as well? I'm trying to do a bit of schedule juggling so Tristan and I can both leave at five.

Violet: Of course, no problem. Adriana has cross-country until six-thirty again, so there's no rush for me to get home.
So how's the fake fiancé thing going, by the way?!
Jesus, when Tristan told me, it was all I could do not to spit coffee all over him. I can't believe the man has no clue you've got a thing for him.

Zoey: Neither does anyone else!
You just have super-powered crush-sniffing abilities.

Violet: Ugh. I do. A hazard of raising three daughters. With all four of us dating now, it's like a romance war zone around here. Someone's always falling in love, falling out of love, or getting her heart ripped—still beating—from her chest. I'm honestly looking forward to the day when I'm finally too old to hunt for Mr. Right.

Zoey: You're never too old for love! You just need to find the right guy.

Violet: I just need to find A guy. Period. At my age, you can't be too picky, honey. Not a whole lot of great catches out there between the ages of forty and fifty.

Zoey: Well, if there is one, you'll sweep him off his feet. You're gorgeous and funny and you make the most amazing pottery I've ever seen. My flamingo mug is seriously the highlight of my morning, every morning.

Violet: You're sweet. And it's adorable that you think I'll be this easily distracted from getting the goods on you and the boss man.
Spill it, sweetheart. I need details!

Zoey: There's not a whole lot to tell. I had to head home right after dinner to give the ferrets their last doses of antibiotics. But I guess things did get a little...interesting before dinner.

Violet: Interesting? What kind of interesting?

Zoey: Oh, you know, just...interesting.

Violet: Fine, keep your secrets, sunshine. I should have known better than to ask. You are the most tight-lipped kid I've ever met. I swear, Tristan gossips more than you do.

Zoey: I'm sorry. I can't help it. I'm just not the type to kiss and tell.

Violet: Oh boy... So, you kissed him, then?!
Was it amazing? Everything you'd dreamed it would be and more?
Send one eggplant emoji for no, two for yes—that way you're not technically kissing and telling. You're communicating in non-verbal emoji code.

Zoey: *one eggplant emoji* *second eggplant emoji*

Violet: YAY!! DOUBLE EGGPLANT!! I'M SO HAPPY FOR YOU SWEETIE! You two are going to be so adorable together! I knew the day would come when that sweet, handsome idiot would finally open his baby browns and see the treasure sitting right outside his office.

Zoey: Oh no, it's not like that, Vi. It's still just a fake relationship.

I mean, I could tell Tristan enjoyed the kiss, too, but for now, that's all it was—a kiss that led to me getting fired, followed by a nice dinner, and a semi-awkward hug goodbye.

Violet: WHAT? HE FIRED YOU?!

How could he fire you? Does he have his head shoved completely up his ass? You're the best thing to happen to this shelter in twenty years!

Zoey: Calm down, Vi. It's okay.

Violet: I will not calm down. And it's not okay! Believe me, I used to volunteer here back before the board put Tristan in charge and he hired competent support staff. It was a nightmare. And I honestly don't care how nice he usually is, this is completely out of bounds!

Zoey: Just wait a second, okay?

Violet: I'm flabbergasted! That he thinks he can get away with this! That he thinks he can fire you a day after sweet-talking you into pretending to be his fiancée without facing consequences for his actions. That's grounds for a lawsuit right there, honey, and I'm not going to stand by and let you—

Zoey: VIOLET PLEASE LET ME EXPLAIN!

Violet: Okay… Fine…
No need to shout…

Zoey: Tristan did fire me, but only so he could re-hire
me in a different position.
That's why I texted you about the scheduling. From
now on, I'm the one in charge of schedules, payroll, and
budget.

Violet: Oh my God…
You mean…

Zoey: I'm the boss. Tristan promoted me and demoted
himself to my position. Starting tomorrow morning, the
corner office is mine.

Violet: Christ…
Well, you know what this means, don't you?

Zoey: That he's insane?

Violet: That he's got it bad for you!!! So bad he's willing
to give up the corner office to eliminate any worries
about potentially taking advantage of his position!
Honestly, I think it's the most romantic thing I've
ever heard.

Zoey: No, Violet. As much as a part of me would like to
believe that, this is just the way Tristan is. He's a rule-
follower and a gentleman, and this is the only way he
could see to handle a situation that was blurring the

lines too much for his comfort. He probably also has a touch of OCD. I've always suspected he might, but after seeing how clean his house is, I'm convinced of it. No single man's house is that clean and meticulously organized. Even the dog-toy area was tidy.

Violet: This is love, Zoey, not OCD.

Zoey: Now who's crazy?

Violet: You are. Or blind. Just wait, I bet your new assistant is asking you out on a real date before the week is through.

Zoey: Not a fair bet. We've already got a date for Wednesday, remember? That's why I texted you in the first place. And it's not a *real* date, it's a picnic in the square on concert night, when everyone in town will be out and about. It's a chance to prove to our exes that we're disgustingly in love. That's it.

Violet: Keep telling yourself that, sweetie. But don't be surprised when he makes his move. And don't let him slip through your fingers. You deserve happiness with a wonderful guy who adores you.

Zoey: I still think you're crazy, but…thank you. See you Wednesday.

Violet: See you then, but feel free to text tomorrow if you have any exciting developments you need to share.

Or swing by after work and join us for supper if you need to spill the good stuff in person.

Zoey: I thought you had enough relationship drama at your house already.

Violet: Oh, but there's always room for more, honey. With love, there's always room for more.

CHAPTER 7

TRISTAN

I'm out of my mind.

I have lost my marbles and should seek professional help as soon as possible. I write "get a referral to a therapist" on my calendar for next week, humming as I toss the pen back onto the desk and grab Luke's leash. I'm heading to work thirty minutes early so I can get the coffee started in the break room and pull paperwork for the morning adoptions—jobs that only yesterday belonged to my assistant. In fact, I'll be getting to the shelter early and leaving late for the foreseeable future for a grand total of two thousand dollars less per month than I was making before.

True, money isn't everything, and I was lucky enough to have bought my house during a dip in the market, enabling me to pay it off last year. Even with my car payment, my monthly expenses are relatively low, and it's not like I have any urge to lead a more lavish lifestyle. My idea of a big weekend involves a long bike ride down a country road, a trip to the farmer's market, and a bottle of wine shared with friends and family in my backyard or at my dad's farm.

And it's not like my job will change all that much—except that I'll be spending less time with numbers and budgets and more time with the animals that are the reason I took a position with A Better Way shelter in the first place.

In fact, the more I ponder the new order of things, the more...*not* crazy it seems.

By the time I pull into the parking lot, my dog happily squirming in the passenger's seat beside me, I've decided to scratch that therapist call off the list as soon as I get home.

If it's madness to be content swapping more joy for less money, then I guess I'll just have to let my crazy flag fly with pride.

Besides, Boss Lady looks good on Zoey. I round reception to see her re-arranging my old desk, a pencil jabbed into the messy bun atop her head, and can't help but smile.

Damn, she's sexy. Even in a pair of jeans and a tight tee covered by a weathered blue flannel. And now I don't have to feel like a creep for discreetly admiring the curve of her ass in those jeans...

"There you are." She bustles out of the office with a stern look on her face and her hands propped on her hips. "We have to talk."

"All right." I set my keys on her old desk as Luke welcomes her with a full-body wag. "What's on your mind, boss?"

Her forehead furrows. "That. The boss thing. I've been thinking about it all night, Tristan, and it just doesn't make sense."

I cock my head. "It makes sense to me. Now you're my boss and I'm your employee. Therefore, I don't have to worry that I'm abusing my position with the fake fiancée business. Problem solved."

"But the fake fiancée thing is only until January," she says. "And swapping our positions really doesn't change anything. Except that now *I'm* the boss and the one who could be accused of abusing her position of power."

My lips curve. "It's okay. I promise. I'm not going to sue you."

"Well, I wasn't going to sue you, either." She crosses her arms with a huff. "And this isn't funny. I'm serious. Not to mention that this could all be solved by drafting a comprehensive policy condoning consensual interoffice relationships and running it past the board during the next meeting. I mean, I know that doesn't exactly cover our situation exactly, but it's close enough."

"See, you're already proving to be a superior leader," I say, smile widening as Luke enthusiastically licks her hand in agreement. "You've got a plan already for a long-term solution."

"Not that long term." Her eyes plead with me to see reason. "The board meets next month. This could all be taken care of in a few weeks, and you wouldn't have to be demoted for no reason. You're so good at your job, Tristan, and I don't feel—"

"Thank you," I cut in, as Luke rubs his head repeatedly against Zoey's thigh, clearly wanting more of her attention than he's getting. "But I'm not sure I love my job as much as I did a few years ago, back before the business side of things got so overwhelming and I ended up spending half my time in front of my computer. The past six months, the budget cuts, the fundraiser to make up for the budget cuts, all the new forms from the state and the talking with the lawyers about the forms—it's been a lot. I miss being hands-on with the animals."

"Even the stool sample part?" She cocks her head, brows raised.

"Even the stool sample part. So as long as you want the promotion and think you can handle it—I, for one, absolutely know you can—I think we should give this new arrangement a shot. At least until after the New Year."

Zoey sighs, relief softening her features, even though Luke is circling her like a shark in his desperation to be petted. "And then you'll take your job back?"

"If you really want me to, I will. Yes. But in the meantime, I have to respectfully disagree with you that the ethical situation is the same," I say, dropping my volume. "Yes, a woman could technically sexually harass her male assistant, but we all know it doesn't usually work that way. I absolutely feel more comfortable knowing you're free to be a part of the fake fiancé plan because you truly want to be a part of it, not out of any concern for your job or position."

"Luke, go lie down, buddy." Zoey wipes her hand on her jeans with an exasperated sigh as Luke nearly knocks her over in his attempts to steal focus. "Lie down," she repeats, sending Luke slinking away to his corner.

As soon as my love-struck dog departs, Zoey darts a quick look toward the still empty reception room before stepping closer. "If this is all because of the kiss last night, Tristan, it really isn't necessary. I didn't feel sexually harassed or pressured to do anything I didn't want to do. Honestly. It's all good."

"Good." I hold her gaze, fighting to keep my focus off her lips and my thoughts away from how much I already want to kiss her again. Sending her on her way after dinner last night without another taste of her was fucking torture. "And this shift in operations will help keep it that way. Now, if you'll excuse me, boss, I need to go take that stool sample from Marvin's litter box."

"You're so darned stubborn," Zoey says, shaking her head.

"And you're beautiful," I say, the words out before I can think better of them.

She rolls her eyes to the ceiling as her cheeks go pink. "Yeah, right. In my garage-sale flannel and my jeans from high school."

"In your garage sale flannel and jeans from high school," I repeat in a steady voice, every cell in my body aching to pull her into my arms and show her just how beautiful I think she is.

How sexy.

How damn-near irresistible.

This fake relationship is veering off the rails at the speed of a bullet train, but maybe that's...all right.

Maybe it doesn't matter that it took a little bit of

pretend to make me realize I have very real feelings for Zoey. It's not just lust with her; it's already so much more. I want to get closer to her in every way, to slip through her defenses and get to the heart of this often deeply private woman. I want to know what makes her tick. The silly things that make her happy, the secret things that make her sad, and the erotic things that make her fall apart when she's naked in my bed.

God, I want that. So fucking much...

Keeping my hands to myself is torturous, especially when she's looking at me the way she is right now, like she wouldn't be opposed to being kissed senseless. Her lips are parted, her breath is coming faster, and I can already taste how sweet her mouth will be beneath mine.

I step closer, a heartbeat away from wrapping an arm around her waist and drawing her close, when a distant snapping sound—like the crunch of giant bone snapping in two—fills the air.

Zoey and I both curse before simultaneously launching into motion.

I lead the way with her close behind, racing down the back hallway, out the door, across the yard, and up the stairs to her apartment.

As expected, the door to Zoey's place has once again been demolished by a bad dog with a breaking and entering problem. The only thing that remains to be seen is whether we've reached Luke before he managed to ingest any of Zoey's clothing.

"No, Luke!" I shout, sprinting through the doorway and lunging for the dog, who is already chewing frantically on something lavender and lacy. "Stop that, bad dog!"

I wrap an arm around his neck and press my finger and thumb into the thick muscles of his jaw, squeezing just hard enough to get him to drop whatever he's on the verge of devouring, hopefully sparing us another trip to the vet and possible surgery.

The fabric falls from his slobbery mouth and Zoey is there to snatch it up with a moan of dismay. "Oh, Luke. What are we going to do with you, buddy? This was my best bra."

I glance over, brows lifting as I take in the ripped lace dangling from Zoey's fingers, suddenly even angrier at my poorly behaved pooch. I know it's a long shot, and Zoey and I might very well end up staying nothing more than friends, but something primal inside of me is keening at the moon, mourning the loss of the chance to see Zoey's breasts cradled in purple lace.

"I'm sorry," I say, clearing my throat when the words come out sounding huskier than I would like. "I'll replace it. We'll order you a new one online during lunch."

Zoey shakes her head. "No, it's fine. It was old, anyway. But I guess I'm going to have to get a steamer trunk with a lock on it instead of drawers. Something the sock-and-panty bandit can't open with his paws."

"No, what you need is a door that's not going to give out every time a hundred and forty pounds of dog lunges at it." I stand, releasing Luke, who rolls over on his back, presenting his belly in a show of contrition. "If Luke can get in, so could a human intruder with less innocent intentions. I'm going back to the board and insisting they spring for a heavyweight security door. Better yet, I'll spring for it, get it installed, and then send them the invoice."

"There's no need for that," Zoey says, reaching out to scratch Luke's belly. "I'm safe here. Seriously, I'm more worried about coyotes than I am human bad guys."

"Well, I'm worried about them, and I'm worried about you," I say, refusing to let her blow this off. "This has gone on long enough. Until I can get a suitable door in place, this isn't a safe situation for you or your clothing." I pace the width of her tiny living room, deliberately keeping my gaze from the full bed on the far side of the studio apartment. "So, until it can be made safe, I think you should come stay with me."

Zoey's brows shoot up. "With you?"

"In my guest room," I clarify. "It's got a lock on the door, and the hall is too narrow for Luke to get a running start at it. He won't be able to break in, you and your underthings will be safe until we get the security door installed here, and if we run into Kim and Bear, it will look like we're living together—it's a win, win, win situation."

"Except for you," she says, gazing down at her hand as it threads through Luke's golden fur. "Won't you miss your privacy?"

"No, Zoey, I won't miss my privacy. I like having you around."

She looks up, her lips curving. "Yeah?"

"Yes. So pack your things. You're coming home with me tonight. I'm not taking no for an answer."

"You're awfully bossy for someone who isn't my boss anymore," she teases as she stands. "Are you sure you're going to be okay with not calling the shots?"

"Totally fine with it," I promise her, unable to keep myself from adding, "At work, anyway."

Something sparks in her eyes, curiosity mixed with excitement that sends a bolt of awareness zipping right below my belt. "So you're saying you want to call the shots off the clock, during Operation Fake Fiancé?"

"Something like that," I say, my gaze burning into hers.

Her lips part and a hungry expression flickers across her features—making her look so different than the sweet, innocent Zoey I thought I knew so well—and for a second, I'm positive she's going to make a move.

And fuck if the thought of Zoey reaching for me, taking what she wants, isn't sexy as hell. I'm instantly harder, thicker, ready to give her everything she wants and more, but before the tension building between us can reach the breaking point, a deep voice calls from outside, "Tristan, you up there? It's Deacon."

I momentarily consider hiding out until my big brother goes away, but Luke is already breaking into joyous barks and dashing for the ruined door.

"There you are, Luke," Deacon says from the bottom of the steps. "Where's your daddy?"

Cursing silently, I take a step back. "I better see what's up. Deacon wouldn't drive all the way out here without a good reason."

Zoey nods, running a hand over her ponytail. "Of

course. I'll just...clean up and lock up as best I can and be down in a few."

Hating to leave her even for a few minutes—proving I'm definitely developing something more serious than a crush—I force myself to turn and hurry down the stairs.

Deacon looks up, lifting a hand to shield his eyes from the morning sun. "Luke broke down Zoey's door again, I see."

"Yeah," I say with a sigh. "I'm going to get a security door in there this time. Something strong enough even a lovesick dog fueled by fantasies of delicious socks can't break through."

Deacon grunts, his blue eyes crinkling at the edges. "Or you could try the hardcore obedience school over in Bennett Valley. I hear they work wonders with cases like Luke. It's like military school for dogs. Whip the mischief right out of him."

"Like the Air Force whipped it out of you?" I cast my brother a pointed look, making him laugh.

"Well, it might at least mellow Luke out a bit." He nods toward the parking lot. "Speaking of mellowing out, that's why I'm here. Dad asked me to stop by on my way into Healdsburg to pick up a load of wine barrels for Emma. He finally figured out what's wrong with your psycho cow."

"Moo-donna isn't psycho," I say, coming to her defense. "She just doesn't like Dylan's attitude. He's the only one she's ever bitten. She can tell he doesn't like her, and she's letting him know the feeling's mutual."

Deacon shoves his hands in his jean pockets,

following me across the yard to the paddock, where our small herd of rescue horses is eagerly awaiting their morning grain. I circle around the fence toward the shed, figuring I might as well make myself useful while bringing Deacon around to my way of seeing things.

"That may be so," he says as I work the combination lock, "but she's been cranky with Dad lately, too. Off her feed, bellowing a lot, and just generally miserable to live with. I told Dad she reminded me of Christy when she was pregnant with the twins, so he got the vet out to check and...sure 'nuff."

"You're kidding," I say, pulling the lock open. "How?"

"Well, I thought you were past needing that talk, but when a boy cow and a girl cow have a special sleepover, sometimes—"

"Ha, ha, jackass. I meant that Moo-donna is always on our property and we don't have any bulls. Kind of hard to have a special sleepover without a male in the picture."

"Apparently she got loose sometime last spring and went for a little walkabout. Dad ended up finding her a few miles down the bike trail in someone else's pasture, so he figured no harm, no foul and it would be best not to tell you that he'd nearly lost your pet. But apparently Moo-donna enjoyed a night of passion while she was free and now you're going to have two new mouths to feed."

I huff with laughter. "No way. Twins?"

Deacon grins. "Must be something in the water over there at the farm. Christy and I were living with Dad

68

when she got pregnant with the boys, too, and there's not a history of twins in either of our families."

"Maybe I shouldn't have taken that demotion, after all," I joke as I open the shed door, stepping into the cool interior to grab the grain bucket. "If I'm going to be buying feed for three once the kids are weaned."

Deacon follows me inside, grabbing the spare bucket. "What do you mean? When were you demoted?"

"I demoted myself last night so there wouldn't be a professional conflict of interest with Zoey and I pretending to be together. Now she's in charge, and I'm taking orders."

He grunts. "Really? And how's that going so far, Mr. Control Freak?"

"I'm only a control freak when I doubt the leadership of the person in charge." I step back out into the morning sun, headed for the troughs, where the horses are already gathered expectantly, used to the morning routine by now. "I don't doubt Zoey's abilities for a second. She could run this entire place by herself if she had to. She's worth two of me."

"I doubt that," Deacon says, "but I've always enjoyed your humble side, baby brother. It's a nice contrast to the two cocky turds who came before you."

I grin. "Dylan isn't cocky, he just puts on an act when he's nervous."

"True, but Rafe has always thought very well of himself."

"He has," I agree. "I don't know how Carrie puts up with him."

"Carrie thinks well of herself, too. They're a perfect pair."

"Morning, Deacon," Zoey calls out, waving a hand from the other side of the pen.

"Morning," he calls back.

"I got the door pieced together as best I could, Tristan," Zoey says, "and put the old bookcase in front of it that we used to block Luke's access last time. Do you want me to put him in a kennel to keep him out of trouble? Or let him out into the dog run with the others for morning exercise?"

"You can let him out into the dog run," I say. "He's playing well with the rest of them now that the bulldog with the bad attitude got adopted last week. But remember, you're the boss. You don't have to ask for my two cents before you make a call."

She rolls her eyes. "I do when it's your dog, you crazy person. See you inside. Bye, Deacon. Have a good one."

Deacon waves goodbye, a shit-eating grin on his face that makes my lips twist.

"What?" I demand as I fill the shorter trough. "What's the grin about?"

"Speaking of perfect matches…" He dumps his grain into the next trough over. "You two are both such solid, generous, hard-working people. Can't really imagine a better fit, honestly. The only thing that bothers me is why I didn't see it the first time I met the girl. Or why it took you three years to kiss her."

"You're ridiculous," I say. "I'm not talking about this anymore with you."

But is he really ridiculous, when he's echoing thoughts that have been dancing through my head non-stop since last night?

I don't know, but I don't regret asking Zoey to move in with me for a second, even if it will be hell keeping things friendly while exposed to her sexy self all day at work and all evening after hours.

Hell, but what a sweet vision, and one I'm looking forward to far more than I should.

CHAPTER 8

*H*e only asked me to move in because it's practical.

My door is broken, his place is close to work, and having me in residence gives Project Fake Fiancé additional street cred. After all, if Tristan and I were really desperately in love and planning a spring wedding, we'd surely already be living together. Bear and I moved into his off-campus apartment three months after we started dating, and we never even got close to "I do."

That's all this is—a practical choice.

But as I follow Tristan up the front steps and through his front door, my heart is pounding and my stomach feels like someone set up a wind farm in there.

Seven days...

I'll be staying with Tristan for at least the next seven days—the absolute earliest the hardware store said they would be able to deliver and install the extra-heavy-duty new door—and I'm way more excited about that than I should be.

Oh, the trouble we could get into in seven days...

Lots and lots of trouble, I'm thinking. Especially if the suspicion that's been tickling my brain all day is founded.

Either I'm completely losing it, or Tristan was flirting with me this morning. After his brother left, we got too busy for banter—our volunteers arrived, and we were slammed with adoption meetings and unexpected drop-offs—but the vibe when we were alone together was definitely *not* purely friendly. Like when he said he was fine with me being in charge and then added, *at work*, in a voice so sexy I could no longer be held responsible for the state of my panties, for example.

I seriously thought I was going to faint. Faint, or pounce on him and beg him to boss away. Boss me up, boss me down, boss me flat onto my back and hold me down hard while he does absolutely anything he wants to my body.

Oh, the wicked imaginings those two little words sent flooding through my mind. All day long, I've had graphic, stomach-flutter-inducing fantasies about Tristan locking his fingers around my wrists, Tristan fisting his hand in my hair, Tristan taking charge and taking me in a way that leaves no doubt that he wants me every bit as much as I want him.

That's the core of the fantasy, after all, the thrill of imagining what it would be like to know Tristan wants me so much he's powerless to resist, no matter how hard he might try to be a gentleman.

"Ready to see your room?" Tristan casts a friendly glance at me over his shoulder as he drops his keys and wallet in a dish by the door, clearly having no idea I've been daydreaming for hours about getting him naked.

I force an equally not-sex-starved expression onto my face and nod. "Sure. That would be great."

"I'll need to get some sheets from the cupboard, but otherwise everything should be ready for you." Tristan leads the way down the hall, opening a door on the left, revealing the room I didn't get a peek into yesterday. Immediately, my eyes begin to tingle pleasantly from the combination of soft yellow walls and a bright floral bedspread featuring giant peonies in various shades of orange, red, and yellow.

"It's gorgeous." I step inside, dragging my roller suitcase behind me. Luke jumps over the purple hard shell in his excitement to beat Tristan and me inside and begins gamboling back and forth around the bed. He's clearly thrilled to have me here, and I can't help wishing his master was equally easy to read.

But Tristan's got his "just friends" face on, again, making me wonder if I imagined that moment of heat and connection in my apartment.

It's possible, I guess…

The thought is enough to dim my excitement a watt or two.

"Are you sure?" Tristan asks, his brow furrowing. "I have another bedspread in the closet if this one is too loud. I like it, but Kim's mom said it gave her a headache. When she came to visit, we had to swap it out for something calmer."

I shake my head and wave a hand in the air. "No, no, it's great, I love it. Really. It's not too loud at all." I scrunch my nose. "So, what's it like? Living in the house you used to share with your fiancée? Is that weird at all?"

Tristan shrugs. "A little bit weird. At first. But now I don't think about it much. Kim and I were together when I bought the house, but she didn't move in until a year later. So in a way, I guess it's always felt more like mine than ours. I do miss her mom, though. Karen did her share of complaining, but she also made the most incredible chicken pot pie."

I nod, unable to resist adding in a smug voice, "Oh, I'm sure it was great pot pie. But I can betcha I can do better. And it'll be a vegetarian version that harms no living thing aside from some succulent late summer veggies."

"Oh yeah?" A challenging smile flashes across his face. "Is that so?"

"It's absolutely so." I drum my fingertips together in front of my face, evil genius style. "In addition to creating perfectly sweaty socks, irresistible to all dogkind, I'm also an accomplished home cook."

Tristan bites his lip and shakes his head, faking a turned-on moan that I desperately wish was the real thing. "Well, damn, girl, I've got leftover roasted vegetables in the fridge and flour in the pantry. Let's see you work some magic."

"That's nice, but I'm going to need cornmeal," I say, laughing when he lets out an over-the-top gasp of surprise. "Yes, I use cornmeal. And if we can find some okra still lingering on a shelf somewhere, I'm going to take those bad boys along for the vegetarian pot pie ride."

Tristan nods firmly. "To the store, then. I'll grab bags, you make your list, and I'll meet you at the front door in five."

I salute him as he crosses to the door. "Yes, sir."

He pauses in the doorway, turning back to me with a heated look in his eyes. "See? Sleepovers are fun, right?"

I nod, trying not to let all the ways I'd like to sleep-over—and under—him show on my face. "They are."

"And it's going to get even better. After dinner, I've got a surprise for you."

"What kind of surprise?" I ask, eyes narrowing as Luke comes to lean against my side, clearly ready to assist me in making my list of ingredients or unpacking my socks or anything else I might need help with.

Tristan's brows bob up and down. "The surprising kind. You'll find out after dinner. But I'll give you a hint —it involves role-playing and will absolutely get us ready to rock our first public appearance as a couple tomorrow night."

"Sounds good," I say, but that's only half true.

The role-playing part definitely sounds interesting, but I'm not sure how I feel about more "practicing" to be a couple. More than ever, I want to know what it would be like to be the woman in Tristan's life for real. To be the person who ambles across the square to the health food store with him, gets messy with him in the kitchen making supper, and hears his appreciative, oh-so-satisfied moans of delight as he devours my latest home chef experiment and goes back for seconds.

And, of course, to make him moan for other reasons, too...

* * *

As we clean up after dinner, bumping into each other in the galley-style kitchen as we hand-wash pots and load the dishwasher, every innocent brush of his arm against mine sets off a mini-supernova of desire.

I don't know if it's the delicious meal, the sexy Motown music playing on the stereo, or memories of yesterday's kiss that assault my senses every time I allow my gaze to slide down to Tristan's lips, but by the time we're finished tidying up, I'm in a seriously over-stimulated state.

Or under-stimulated...

That's all this is—a completely natural reaction to being thrust into constant contact with my sexy boss after three years of sensual deprivation. I'm like a bear fresh out of hibernation, lean and hungry and intoxicated by the scent of every fresh spring berry popping out on the vine. I am a bear, Tristan is an innocent mountain blackberry, and I should definitely go straight to bed—alone—do not role-play, do not engage in couple practice, do not risk revealing how much I want this fantasy to become a reality.

But when Tristan takes my hand and nods toward the living room, where he's started the first fire of autumn in the fireplace, I can't help but follow. I usually consider myself a level-headed, self-disciplined woman, but this man makes me want to throw caution to the wind and reach for what I want, what I need, with both hands.

CHAPTER 9

TRISTAN

"What's all this?" Zoey stops dead at the edge of the living room, eyes going wide as she spots the impromptu picnic I set up in front of the fireplace. It's not much—just one of my mom's old quilts spread out on the floor with dessert waiting in the middle—but the flickering firelight makes the setting more romantic than I anticipated.

But that's perfect. The concert in the square tomorrow night will be romantic, too—best to put our faking-it skills to the test in a similar environment.

"I thought we could combine business and pleasure," I say, squeezing her hand, enjoying holding it more than I probably should. "Dessert and couple practice."

"Oh. Wow. Well, that cheesecake looks amazing, but honestly, I'm so stuffed I don't think I could eat another bite."

"Me, either. But I don't regret going back for seconds. You knocked Mrs. Kahn's lame-o pot pie out of the park." Releasing her hand, I start for the blanket. "So I'll pop the cake back in the fridge and be right back. Make yourself comfortable and start thinking about all the annoying shit I do that pisses you off."

Zoey huffs softly in surprise. "That pisses me off?"

"The things that really make you want to wrap your fingers around my throat and squeeze," I toss over my shoulder as I ferry dessert back to the kitchen.

When I return, Zoey is settled on the quilt with her shoes off and her legs tucked beneath her. The firelight catches her hair, bringing out streaks of red I haven't noticed before, and her face glows in the pink and orange light. She looks like something out of a painting, so beautiful it's almost heartbreaking. Looking at her now, as I settle onto the blanket beside her, I can't think of a single thing I would change about this woman, let alone anything about her that drives me crazy.

"This is going to be harder than I thought," I confess, suddenly nervous.

"Why?" Zoey asks. "What are we practicing? Yelling at each other?"

"Sort of," I say with a laugh. "I was thinking today about what it's like to be a couple. Like, what are the things that show two people are really and truly together for the long haul. And yes, kissing and holding hands and lingering looks are all a part of it, but so is the flip side of being in an intimate relationship."

"Fighting..." Zoey supplies with a frown, clearly unconvinced.

"You don't agree? You and Bear never argued?"

She blinks, her brows lifting. "No, we did. I guess.

Sometimes. He liked to watch reality TV, and I preferred Masterpiece Classic, so we'd clash over who got to control the remote every once in a while. And he thought it was weird that I eat pizza with a fork and knife, and he drove me crazy throwing his dirty clothes on the floor near the hamper instead of actually *inside* the hamper. But...nothing too intense. We never really had a big blow up. Even when we broke up."

I *humph* beneath my breath. "Really? Never?"

She shakes her head, making her ponytail swish. "No. Never."

"But you would say you had a passionate connection in other ways?" I ask, pushing on when her gaze darts uncomfortably to the fire. "Not to pry, I'm just curious, I guess. Kim and I fought all the time, but I assumed that was just part of having an intense relationship. But I could be wrong. I honestly don't have much dating experience aside from nearly a decade with a girl I hooked up with while we were both still in high school." I shrug. "It could have been that our relationship was immature or something."

"You're not immature," Zoey says. "Not even a little bit. You're one of the most grounded, responsible men I know."

"Thank you." I hold her gaze, fighting the urge to lean in and kiss her. It's her first night here as my houseguest, and I'm still not sure where we stand as far as being something more than friends.

Could she want more than pretend, too? Yes, she seems attracted to me, but neither of us have put real-life dating on the table, and my gut says it's better to play it safe than to push too soon and scare her away.

"And you might have a point," Zoey continues, skimming her fingers over the quilt where a patch of bright red fabric meets a faded flower print. "Bear and I were good together, and I loved him, but I wouldn't say our relationship was all that intense or passionate. I was actually okay when he ended things. Sad, but okay." She lets out a long breath. "But I've seen some of my friends go through breakups that truly devastated them. They were so miserable and down that I worried about their safety." Zoey glances up at me through her long lashes. "Like you, right after Kim left. You were so sad it hurt to look at you."

My chest goes tight. "I'm sorry."

"Why are you sorry? You were sad. It's okay to be sad."

"I know, but I'm still sorry. I hate that I worried people." I shake my head slightly. "And I hate that I was so fucking pathetic for so long."

Zoey's hand comes to rest lightly on my cheek, her soft touch making the ache in my chest even worse. "You weren't pathetic. You were heartbroken, and there's no shame in that. Though, it did make me want to break the face of the woman who'd hurt you. And that was before I knew you'd been dumped by Kim-gis Khan."

My lips curve. "Kim-gis Khan?"

"Like Ghengis Khan." Zoey's fingers slide up, brushing my hair from my face, making the moment feel even more intimate. "She slaughtered her enemies with words, he slaughtered his with swords, but I always thought they had a lot in common aside from the last name."

"Slaughtered, huh?" I arch a brow. "If that's what you call 'kid stuff' I'd hate to see what you consider a full-fledged, grown-up offense."

Zoey wrinkles her nose and her hand drops back to the quilt. "Yeah, that might be a strong word. But the point is, I get why you were sad. You had something intense and it ended. I just haven't been there yet, myself. So, if we're going to have a lover's quarrel, you're going to have to teach me how to pull it off."

"Are you sure?" I ask. "Maybe this is a stupid idea."

"No, it's not stupid. I get what you're saying, and it sounds like seeing us fighting might convince Kim we're living happily ever after more than making goo-goo eyes at each other ever will." She shifts onto her knees, palms resting on her thighs. "So, let's do this. Show me how to fight."

I smile at her prim prepared-for-battle stance, but nod. "Okay, so I figured it would be best to start with at least a kernel of something real. That will make faking a blow up easier and more believable. So, tell me, what drives you nuts about me?"

Zoey blinks, shakes her head, and sighs. She puckers her lips, furrows her brow, and sighs again. She crosses her arms, taps a finger to the side of her mouth, and hums soft and low.

"That many things, huh?" I tease, making her grin.

"No, not that many things. Not anything at all, really.

Except…" She trails off with a nervous laugh and a shrug.

"Except what?"

She waves a hand between us as if to dismiss the topic. "Nothing, it's nothing."

"No, tell me," I press. "Seriously, I can take it, Zoey. I'm a big boy. What gets on your last nerve? Tell me."

She looks up, eyes going wide. "No. I can't."

"Tell me," I insist, letting heat creep into my voice as I see a perfect opening and go for it. "Why is getting you to open up such a battle?"

Zoey's brows shoot up. "Me? You're the one who's a locked book."

"A locked book?"

"Like an open book, but the opposite," she says, utterly serious. "A book that's locked up and determined to keep all his secrets."

I'm tempted to laugh at the description, but I force myself to keep up the angry act. "Oh yeah? Like what? What have you ever wanted to know that I haven't been willing to talk about?"

"All kinds of things!" she says, volume building. "Like after your breakup, you refused to talk or let anyone in. You just trudged around looking stoic and losing weight so fast I couldn't stop making sandwiches for you and leaving them in the staff fridge with your name on them. And after Smoky died, too. You didn't talk or cry; you just ghosted for days."

"I was at work the next day," I say, a pang of real irritation zipping through me. Smoky, our old office cat, who'd roamed between my desk and Zoey's until he'd gotten too stiff to move from his bed near Luke's, had been mine since I found him half-drowned in a ditch when I was sixteen. Losing him had been hard, but I certainly hadn't "ghosted" afterward.

"Your body was there, but your heart wasn't," Zoey said. "Anytime you feel vulnerable, you shut down. You retreat inside your shell and refuse to come out until you're all better. And that sucks."

"Why does it suck?" I ask with a sharp exhalation. "What's wrong with that? I'm trying to be respectful, Zoey. To handle my own shit so other people don't have to."

"So other people don't *get* to," she says in a softer voice. "You do realize that's something friends like to do for each other, right? Help the people they care about handle their shit? Not only does it feel good to be there for someone when they need you, but it lets you know it's okay to reach out to your friend when you need help with your own shit."

I pause, brow furrowing. "You can reach out any time you need help. I'm always here, any time you need me. I hope you know that."

"I know you mean that, but it doesn't feel true sometimes," she says gently. "Being vulnerable isn't a one-way street, Tristan. If both people aren't willing to let down their guard, then the relationship eventually gets weird and uneven. One person becomes the taker, and the other the giver. Or, in our case, no one is the taker or the giver because you're not willing to open up and I'm not willing to ask for help unless I know I'm going to get the chance to be the helper somewhere down the line."

We sit still in the silence following her words, the only sound the crackle of the fire and the soft hiss of the slightly green wood as it burns.

Finally, she leans forward and whispers, "How was that for a fight?"

I pull in a breath as I rub a hand over my jaw. "Good. Less dramatic and screamy than what I'm used to, but intense. And...honest?"

She hesitates, clearly debating for a moment before she nods. "Yeah. It was. I mean, I didn't intend to go there, but it would be nice if you let people be there for you more. Not me, in particular, if that's not something you're comfortable with. But your brothers, maybe. Or your—"

"Why wouldn't I be comfortable with you? We're friends, right? Good friends?"

She nods. "Yes. We are. But we also work together."

"Well...we're not at work now," I say, pressing my lips together as I consider everything she said. "And I can work on getting out of my shell after hours, as long as you promise to do the same. I want to be there for you, Zoey. That part was honest, too."

"Thanks. I appreciate that." Her cheeks dimple as she fights a smile. "So I guess we've graduated to the making up part of the lovers' quarrel?"

"Unless you want to pout and give me the cold shoulder for a few days to prove that you're right and I'm wrong."

Zoey rolls her eyes. "God, no. Pouting is lame. And

I'm way too old and lazy for it. Besides, I can't remember—"

She's interrupted by a long, mournful howl from downstairs, and I silently curse myself for not starting the tennis match over from the beginning instead of picking up from where Luke left off yesterday.

"Sounds like somebody's ready to come back upstairs," Zoey says with a laugh as she hops to her feet. "I'll go let him out."

"And I'll grab his leash. He's used to a walk after dinner. You're welcome to join us if you want."

"Thanks, but I think I'll stay here," Zoey says, backing toward the stairs to the basement. "Shower and get settled in, start some laundry so I have something to wear to work tomorrow, give you guys some privacy…"

The last thing I want is privacy, but clearly Zoey isn't as up for constant togetherness as I am—something I should remember the next time I start thinking confessing my growing feelings for her is a good idea.

I take Luke for his walk alone and return home to find Zoey's door closed. I complete my nightly routine —starting the dishwasher, locking the doors, and kenneling Luke. Only, bedtime tonight involves catching the dog before he can ingest a small, white sweat sock he managed to drag out of the drier in the basement while my back was turned.

I head back upstairs with Zoey's clean laundry in a basket in my arms. Holding her clothes feels pleasantly intimate, and the excuse to knock on her door is way more exciting than it should be. And when she opens the door in a faded gray T-shirt and pink and gray-striped pajama pants, the sight of her all cozy and ready for bed makes it almost impossible to keep from pulling her into my arms.

Instead, I hold out the laundry, "Luke got into the dryer."

"Oh no," she says, brow furrowing as she takes the basket from me. "I'm so sorry. I was certain there was no way he could open the door on the machine or I would have waited down there until it was finished tumbling. He didn't eat anything did he?"

"No, I got to him in time," I assure her. "And it's not your fault. He's clearly got issues. I'll just be sure to kennel him before you do laundry next time."

"Well, maybe I won't have to. If they get the door installed in a week, I should be fine to wait to do laundry again until I'm back home." Her eyes lift to the ceiling. "I'm honestly embarrassed I didn't have clean laundry ready to pack. Things have been so busy at work lately, I kept putting it off for a lazy day that never seemed to come."

"It's fine. And if you need to use the machine again, that's fine, too," I say, not liking the reminder that her stay might be so short. Which means it's past time for me to go to bed, get my head on straight, and stop thinking about how simultaneously snuggly and sexy Zoey looks in her pajamas. "See you in the morning. If you hear Luke whining, don't worry about it. I'll let him out in the backyard as soon as I get up."

"Or I can," she says. "If I'm up first. I don't mind. I want to help out while I'm here, be a good houseguest."

"You made the one vegetarian pot pie to rule them all. You're already the best houseguest ever."

Zoey grins. "Wait until you taste my veggie shepherd's pie. It's even better."

"So you have a way with all pie, then?"

"All savory pies," she corrects. "And savory tarts. I make a mean Cuban meatless tart and a Greek feta pastry guaranteed to deliver a major M.O."

I arch a brow. "A modus operandi?"

Her cheeks flush as she laughs. "Um, no, a mouth orgasm. Sorry. I forget not everyone is up to date on my weird personal lingo."

"It's fine. I like the lingo, and the food sounds great," I say, playing it cool even as the word "orgasm" goes straight to my misbehaving dick. I take a step back, forcing a friendly smile. "Let me know what ingredients you need, and I'll grab them while I'm shopping for our picnic tomorrow."

Zoey nods, biting her bottom lip in a way that makes me ache to feel her mouth soft and hot against mine. "Sounds great. Good night, Tristan."

"Good night, Zoey. Sleep tight." I turn, willing my feet to keep moving toward my room, away from the increasingly irresistible woman down the hall, toward a bed that feels lonely for the first time in months.

I've been alone for over a year, but I haven't felt lonely in a long time. I've been okay flying solo, focusing on friends and family while my heart healed enough to make dating sound palatable again.

Now, I'm suddenly ready—absolutely, completely, desperately ready—to start something with the one woman who should remain off-limits. If I don't want to risk losing Zoey as a friend or a coworker, I should keep my dick in my pants and my crush on her under wraps.

But as I slide into bed and flick off the light, there's only one thought whispering through my head—some things, like sexy sweet girls with freckles dancing across their noses, are worth the risk.

CHAPTER 10

ZOEY

*B*y the time I wake up the next morning—after way too many hours spent wide-eyed and sleepless, so hyperaware of the beautiful and oh-so-tempting man down the hall that I ended up sewing until the wee hours in hopes that the repetitive work would eventually lull me to sleep—Luke is already whining pitifully in his kennel. Hustling down the stairs, I let him out of his crate and take him outside to the backyard, enjoying the cool air and the faint smell of roses drifting from the neighbor's garden until whistling from the other side of the fence alerts me to the fact that I'm not alone.

Squinting in the dim morning light, I hone in on the orange tree in time to see Bear's brown curls appear over the top of the fence.

Moving fast, I duck back inside the sunroom and whisper to Luke, "Here, boy. Come here, Luke. I've got a new toy for you."

Thankfully, Luke gallops eagerly across the lawn, sparing me an early morning chat with my ex. Shutting the door behind him, I pull the stuffed creature I made from all my already damaged socks from my robe pocket and hold it out to the happily squirming dog. "It's a sock doll, just for you, buddy. Made from my thickest, sturdiest socks, so hopefully you won't be able to tear it apart and eat it."

"You're brilliant," a sleep-rough voice pipes up from the hall as Luke enthusiastically snaps the doll from my hands and trots away to add it to his toy collection in the living room.

I look up to see Tristan in dark blue pajama pants and a tight white T-shirt, sporting an adorably rumpled case of bedhead and holding two cups of coffee, and my heart skips a beat. I tell myself it's because I'm really excited about coffee, but of course, I know better.

"Thanks," I say, accepting the mug. "But don't talk too soon. He might still find a way to tear it apart before lunchtime."

"Nah, it looked solid. Should last at least until dinner." He winks, and I find myself grinning up at him like a fool for a good half minute before I remember that I'm hideous and need curl-taming and teeth-brushing—STAT.

Hiding my mouth behind the steaming mug for protection against possible morning breath, I edge around him. "Guess I should get dressed. Did you want to carpool?"

"I can't today—I've got to leave early to hit the store —but tomorrow for sure." He turns, watching me scurry down the hall with an amused look. "Thanks again for the sock toy. I'm sure you've just made Luke's year."

"My pleasure," I say, beaming like an idiot until I'm safely back in my room and get a good look at myself in the mirror above the bureau. "Jesus, Childers." I wince as I shake my head, causing the rat's nest on the right side of my head to drift into my face. "Way to kill the feminine mystique the first morning."

But Tristan hadn't looked at me like I was a hideous morning beast. He'd looked at me like I was an adorable morning beast.

The knowledge makes me flutter all the way to work and throughout the rest of the day—earning me teasing glances from Violet. She catches me mooning at the water fountain and then again near the new outdoor rabbit pen, where I've somehow managed to get stuck in a daydream while filling a bucket full of pellets bound for the compost heap.

"Oh, you've really got it bad now," she says, nudging me with her elbow and nodding toward the back of the property. "Come on, walk with me. Tell Aunty Violet all about your first sleepover. How many times did you come? Three? Four?"

My jaw drops as I cast a furtive glance over my shoulder toward the main building, making sure we're alone before I turn back to her with a hiss, "Shush! It was nothing like that! We just had dinner and practiced fighting so we'd look believable as a couple. It was completely innocent."

Violet sighs in disappointment as she flips her long black ponytail over her shoulder. "Oh, well. Tonight, then. Tomorrow night at the latest. But you two are totally going to bang if you keep staying with him. Mark my words."

"I don't know about that, but…" I start toward the compost heap with Violet beside me, waiting until we're firmly out of earshot before I add in a softer voice, "When we were practicing arguing last night, we talked about some real stuff, and it was so nice. I feel so much closer to him. Like we're better friends already."

Vi's amber eyes dance. "Friends. Right."

"Yes," I insist. "Friends." I fix my gaze on the trail ahead, fighting a grin. "Friends who maybe want to kiss each other."

She lets out a soft whoop that I nevertheless shush immediately.

"Keep your voice down," I say. "I'm trying to play it cool, but I'm getting the feeling that maybe Tristan is starting to feel it, too. This…pull I've felt for so long."

"About time," Violet says, taking my wrist and pulling me to a stop beside her. "But be careful okay. Make sure you have protection covered."

My cheeks heat as I roll my eyes. "Yes, Mom. I've got it covered, I promise. I've got an IUD."

"Of course you do. I just wanted to make sure. Ever since my oldest had that pregnancy scare last year, I'm handing out birth control pills like candy. I don't want any of my girls having babies until they're in committed relationships and ready for motherhood. I'm not ready to be a grandma at forty, and I don't want any of you to have to make the compromises I did."

"Aw, thanks," I say, the backs of my eyes beginning to sting. "I like being one of your girls."

"Of course, gorgeous." Violet puts her slim but surprisingly strong arm around my shoulders for a quick hug. "You always will be. And you'll always be the good one since the other three are a coven of hellions."

We spend the rest of the walk to the compost heap talking about her three girls' various acts of mischief and rebellion, and by the time we get back to the shelter, Tristan's car is gone and there's a note waiting for me on my new desk.

Gone to kill you a picnic worthy of a culinary master's discerning tastes. Meet me by the snail statue at six. I'll be the guy on the picnic blanket with a feast and a dog who's madly in love with you.

I smile so hard my cheeks start to hurt, but even when Violet laughs and swears, "Tonight, girl! It's going down tonight!" I can't bring myself to stop grinning long enough to shush her.

Maybe I'm crazy or imagining things, but I read possibilities between the lines of Tristan's note. Magical possibilities that leave me floating on air through my closing duties, making me immune to the scent of the doggie piles I gather up in the run and the cantankerous hiss of the new Persian cat who's decided she doesn't like the cut of my jib.

Nothing can get me down, not now, not with all my most secret wishes on the verge of coming true.

CHAPTER 11

ZOEY

*A*fter fighting the snarl of traffic at the one and only roundabout in town—the one that's been under construction for three years and likely won't be finished in my lifetime—I park at Tristan's house, dash in for a quick shower and change of clothes, and then walk the four blocks to the square. I won't have to worry about driving after a couple of glasses of wine, and it's a lovely evening for a walk.

Healdsburg is ridiculously picturesque in the rosy sunset light.

Flowers run rampant over every trellis in town—overflowing planters and spilling over fences to tease passersby with thick bougainvillea blossoms and sun-warmed roses perfuming the Indian Summer air. Every quaint old Victorian I pass has a pumpkin or five on the porch and several families have already inflated their giant black cats and ghost yard ornaments in preparation for Halloween.

It's so warm it's hard to believe the spookiest night of the year is less than a week away. It still feels like summer, and as I turn left on Matheson Street, wandering past tasting rooms staying open late to supply wine to concert goers, and art collectives selling everything from paintings to sunglasses with hand-carved wooden frames and stuffed felt narwhal heads ready to be mounted in a place of honor in your home, it feels like summer will never end.

It will always be a perfect seventy-five degrees as the sun goes down. The evening air will always smell like flowers, fresh-cut grass, wood smoke from the pizza oven down the street, and popcorn and cotton candy from the vendors on the square. Tiny fairy lights will always glitter around the thick trunks of the redwoods shading the bandstand, and Manny Miller and His Big Band will always be playing instrumental versions of old musical theater favorites as couples sway in the dusk, holding each other close for minutes they'll remember forever.

I pause at the corner, waiting for the crosswalk light to change, a shiver rushing across my skin as an almost supernatural awareness settles inside me.

I don't know what's about to happen on this beautiful, perfect night, but I know that it will change my life. After tonight, nothing will be the same. I will be changed forever—for better or for worse.

But as I cross the street with the rest of the crowd, flanked by a tiny silver-haired couple carrying a picnic basket and a young mother holding a giggling, beaming baby who's clearly every bit as enchanted by the evening as I am, I can't imagine anything bad happening tonight.

It's a night for beauty.

A night for relishing the simple, unspeakably precious gift of being alive.

A night for magic...

The thought whispers through my head as my gaze lands on the man camped out on a rainbow-colored quilt beneath one of the square's many statues. Tristan has changed into dark jeans and a white button-down shirt that brings out honey-colored highlights in his olive skin. A bottle of wine chills in a bucket at one corner of the blanket, a picnic basket pins down another, and he and Luke are stretched out in front, listening to the band play with matching sleepy smiles on their faces.

I pause, soaking in the sight of them for a moment before they notice me, my heart overflowing with an emotion I can't quite name. All I know is that looking at them right now, these two feel like home. And as I cross the grass to meet them, for the first time in a long time, I know I'm exactly where I'm supposed to be.

"There you are." Tristan's eyes light up as he sits beside Luke. His gaze flicks down and up, his brows lifting as he takes in my yellow sundress with the daisies embroidered at the hem and simple brown shawl. "Wow. You look...beautiful."

"Thank you," I say, lips curving in a too-wide grin as I settle beside him on the quilt. But I can't seem to help myself. It's been a long time since anyone has looked at me the way Tristan is looking at me right now—like I'm the loveliest woman in the world, the *only* woman in the world—and I can't stop the flush of pleasure that heats my cheeks all the way to the tips of my ears. "I figured tonight might be my last chance to wear a sundress before the nights get too cool, so…"

"It's perfect," Tristan says, making me blush even harder. "You're perfect."

"Thanks," I say, the tension thickening the air between us breaking as Luke drops the sock-stuffy he was holding in his mouth and scoots between us with a whimper, casting a meaningful glance at the picnic basket. "Sorry, Luke. Have you been holding supper for me?" I ask, laughing as he lets out another mournful whimper.

"Enough, drama king." Tristan opens the basket, pulling out a heavy-duty Tupperware container. "We'll feed you first, then, you poor starving animal." He pops the lid on the container and leans back to place it in the grass to the side of the blanket. Instantly, Luke is on his feet, padding around to attack his custom homemade mixture of rice, grilled turkey meat, and fresh veggies.

"You would think I never feed him," Tristan says, shaking his head as Luke digs in with gusto.

I smile. "He's a growing boy, Dad. He needs two meals a day and as many snacks as he can con from easy marks around the office."

"Growing *out* is more like it if he's not careful. He's not a puppy anymore," Tristan says, pulling wineglasses from the basket. "How about you? Are you starving, or would you like a glass of wine before we dig in?"

"A glass of wine sounds lovely." I lean back on my

hands with a happy sigh. "All of this is lovely. The music, the sunset, the people being happy together..." I scan the crowd. From the dancers swaying near the bandstand, to the kids running back and forth across the grass, to the families digging into picnics, nearly everyone has a smile on their face. It's enough to make my already full heart overflow a little. "I love seeing people being so happy together. It gives me hope."

"Me, too," Tristan murmurs. A moment later his lips are warm on my cheek, making my pulse flutter in my throat as I turn to him.

"Is it time?" I whisper. "Are the targets in sight?"

Tristan shakes his head, his face still so close to mine that I can feel the warmth of his skin on my cheeks. I'm drowning in the fresh-soap-and-Tristan scent of him, the one that makes me ache to be even closer to this irresistible man. "No," he says. "It's just because you're you. Is that okay?"

My lashes flutter as my gaze falls to the blanket. "Yes. That's okay." I take a breath, pulse thundering in my ears as I force myself to look up into his warm brown eyes. "It's more than okay, actually."

He searches my face for a moment, his lips parting as if on the verge of making a confession, but before he can speak, something bounces hard onto the blanket between us, nearly knocking over the wine. Tristan grabs the bottle, rescuing our Chardonnay in the nick of time as I reach for the sparkly red ball and glance up, searching for its owner.

Almost immediately, I spot a little boy with chubby cheeks and raven curls, watching me from the grass a few feet away. I hold up the ball, "Is this yours, buddy?"

His eyes go wide as he nods. "Ball," he announces. "Red ball."

"Yes," I agree, taking a moment to appreciate the redness of his ball. "It is very red. That's one of my favorite colors. How about you?"

The toddler grins, clearly delighted as he points behind our blanket. "Snail! Brown snail!"

I laugh, head bobbing with his. "Yes! You are really good with your colors. And your animals." I hold up the ball. "Would you like your ball back?"

He crouches down, holding out his hands as I roll the ball across the grass. The boy snatches it up a second before his dad snatches him into the air, lifting the munchkin into his arms. "Sorry about that," his father says, hugging the boy close with a smile. "We're still working on keeping the ball under control."

"No worries," Tristan says as I smile and agree, "No worries at all. Have fun tonight."

His father wishes us the same and crosses back to his own blanket, which is surrounded by a small flock of folding chairs. There are two little girls with braids coloring in tiny pink chairs, an older boy playing a handheld game in another, and a beautiful woman with thick black curls in a cushy red foldout number, tapping her fingers along to the music on her rounded belly, number five clearly in the works.

"Looks like they have their hands full," I say, turning back to Tristan and accepting a freshly poured glass of Chardonnay.

"Absolutely." He casts another covert glance over my shoulder. "But at least they spaced them out a little more than Dylan and Emma. Their girls are barely ten months apart."

"Irish twins." I blow out a breath as I swirl my wine. "I get tired just thinking about what her day must look like."

"Me, too. Though my brother Deacon swears a shelter full of animals is more work than any number of kids."

I wrinkle my nose. "No way. Animals are easy. Well...relatively easy. Meet their needs for food, shelter, safety, community, and routine and they tick along just fine. It seems like there's so much more that can go wrong with human babies."

Tristan takes a thoughtful drink of his wine, then runs his tongue over his bottom lip, catching a stray drop of liquid and making my heart start fluttering all over again in the process.

He really does have the most beautiful mouth, and any minute now I could be kissing it.

Our plan is to do a little light making out as soon as we spot Kim and Bear, then transition into a disagreement over something work-related, and finish with a more intense kiss-and-make-up session.

I'm nervous about the performance, but I'm even more nervous that I'll *forget* it's a performance... All the lines are blurring with this man, and it's getting harder and harder to separate reality and fantasy.

"I don't know," Tristan finally says as Luke returns to the blanket, flopping down beside me with a satisfied grunt now that his belly is full. "I think human babies need a lot of the same things. Have you thought about kids? If you want them someday? I mean, you're obviously great with them."

I roll my eyes with a laugh. "Oh, I don't know about that. I just happen to have a strong appreciation for red balls and brown snails. Any kind of snail, really. They're pretty fascinating."

"They are," Tristan agrees, his lips curving. "Most species are hermaphrodites."

"I know!" I nod excitedly. "Isn't that wild? I mean, they never know who's going to end up pregnant. Could be Thing One. Could be Thing Two. Could be both of them at the same time..." I sip my wine, nodding as I swallow. "It really gives the whole process a layer of suspense that human reproduction lacks."

Tristan laughs.

"I'm serious," I say, though I can't help smiling. "I sort of wish I was a snail sometimes. Home on your back so you never have to leave it, lots of exciting possibilities every mating season, and even if you end up pregnant you'd only have to lay some eggs under a rock or something, not go through actual childbirth. I confess the thought of growing a life inside of me and then having to get that life *out* safely is pretty terrifying." I clear my throat and take another slightly too-large sip of wine. "What about you? Do you want kids?"

Tristan's grin fades as he lifts a shoulder and lets it fall. "I used to think so. I'm not sure anymore. Not sure I trust myself, I guess."

My brow furrows. "Why? You'd be a great dad.

There's no doubt in my mind. I mean, you're already a stellar dog parent."

"Thanks. Though, with the number of socks Luke's vomited up or had surgically removed from his GI tract, I'm not sure the vet would agree with you." He pats Luke's rump. "Though, that might be behind us now, huh, buddy? Now that you have Zocky."

I grin. "Zocky?"

"A mix of Zoey and sock. It's the perfect name for your brilliant new dog toy. Feel free to use it when you're applying for your patent."

"Will do," I say, nodding soberly. "Thank you so much for the help with that."

"You're welcome." Tristan takes another drink of his wine, making me a little jealous of the rim of his wineglass. "But seriously, he loves it. Zocky's barely been out of his mouth all day. Thank you."

I reach out, scratching Luke's scruff beneath his collar. "Oh, it's my pleasure. I love this crazy mutt, no matter how many socks he's laid waste to through the years."

"He obviously loves you, too," Tristan says, something in his voice making my heart skip a beat. I look over at him, and it lurches into motion again, racing even faster as his hand covers mine. "And I have a confession to make, Zo."

I swallow hard, afraid to hope but unable to stop the soaring, sailing, dreams-coming-true feeling swelling in my chest. "Yes?"

"This pretending to be together thing... It's not..." He shakes his head. "It's just not working out for me."

My soaring hopes plummet so fast the world starts to spin. "Oh, okay." I nod and keep nodding, repeating after a moment. "Okay."

I know I should say something else—something to make the transition back to friends and colleagues easier—but I can't find the words. All I can think is that this might be the last time Tristan's hand is on mine, the last time I get to sit this close to him.

The thought is so horrible and sad that my throat goes tight, and for a second, I'm afraid I might do something mortifying like tear up right here in the middle of the town square. Though I really don't care what any of these people think of me. I only care about him, this man who apparently doesn't feel the pull I feel, doesn't sense the magical possibilities hovering in the wings, waiting for us to reach out and grab them.

"No, it's not okay," Tristan says softly. "I knew it wasn't working out yesterday, and I still went ahead with the fight practice and planning this whole stupid stunt, and I..." His breath rushes out as his fingers curl around mine. "And I shouldn't have. I should have been honest with you the moment I realized that I don't want to pretend with you. I want..."

My eyes go wide as I search his face, afraid to get my hopes up again. But he doesn't look like a man who's getting ready to tell me he wants to be friends. He looks like a man who wants to kiss me and keep kissing me until everything in the world fades away except his lips and mine.

Finally, I summon the courage to ask, "What do you want, Tristan?"

"I want you, Zoey," he says, sending my heart skyrocketing into the darkening sky where it explodes in a burst of dazzling color. "I want to give you and me a shot. For real. If you think you might be up for it."

With a laugh-sob of unadulterated joy, I lean in, pressing my lips to his. He moans softly—a relieved, hopeful, happy sound that echoes everything I'm feeling —and threads his fingers into my hair. His lips part, and his tongue strokes against mine, imprinting the taste of this first *real* kiss indelibly in my memory.

He tastes like butterscotch and oaky Chardonnay with a slight tang of green apple mixed with the sexy, smoky taste of Tristan, and I know I'm never going to forget this moment, this magic, or the way every cell in my body is lighting up with longing and relief. I don't have to hide anymore. I don't have to pretend kissing him isn't the best thing to happen to my mouth in years. I don't have to hold back as I return his kiss, showing him with every brush of skin against skin how grateful I am for this chance to express what he means to me with my touch.

Finally, after a kiss that's probably way too steamy for the town square, we pull apart, breath coming fast. Almost instantly, the square bursts into applause.

And though I know the cheering is for the band's gorgeous take on "The Street Where You Live" from *My Fair Lady*, I can't help but feel like it's meant for us. For this. For the dream coming true under the Sampson the Snail statue.

"So, I assume that's a yes to being my steady date?" Tristan grins as he brushes my hair from my face.

I laugh, lifting my eyes to the pale blue twilight sky. "Yes. Though, I have to say it took you long enough. I've had a thing for you for a while, you know."

"Really?" he asks, seemingly genuinely surprised.

"Yes!" I bite my lip, but I don't want to keep the truth contained. I don't want to hide the way I feel about Tristan ever again. "I'm crazy about you, silly."

"And I've clearly just been crazy." He shakes his head. "I can't believe it took me this long to realize how good this could be. How incredible. Almost as incredible as the way you taste..."

He leans in, but I stop him with two fingers pressed to his mouth. "I can't," I whisper. "No more making out in public tonight."

"Not a fan of public displays of affection?"

"No, I'm just not sure how much longer I'll be able to control myself." I let my fingertip play back and forth across his warm, soft bottom lip. "Kissing you really makes me want to do more than kiss you, Tristan. Like...a lot."

His eyes darken. "I want to do more than kiss you, too. I haven't been able to stop thinking about how much more since the first time we kissed, in fact. But I don't want to rush you, Zoey. We can—"

"Rush me," I whisper, pulse galloping faster as his fingers curl around the back of my neck and desire flashes across his face. "Please, rush me."

"You're sure?" he asks, holding my gaze with an intensity that makes me shiver.

I nod. "Yes. I'm sure. I want you to take me home, Tristan. Right now."

"Grab Luke's leash and get him hooked up," he says, his voice husky. "I'll get everything else packed, and we'll be out of here in five minutes."

Sizzling with anticipation, with urgency, with the euphoria of knowing that I'm about to feel what it's like to be in Tristan's arms, in his bed, with nothing separating his incredible body from mine, I hook Luke's leash to his collar with trembling hands and grab his empty supper dish from the grass. Within moments, Tristan has the picnic basket repacked, the wine corked, the quilt folded and his arm around my waist.

"Let's get home, beautiful." He kisses my cheek again, but this time there's nothing sweet about it. Even in that gentle brush of his lips against my skin, I can feel the erotic possibilities simmering in the air between us, making my body ache and my voice breathy as I say, "I can't wait."

Hand-in-hand, we start down the path leading out of the square, walking fast enough that Luke has to trot to keep up. We reach the crosswalk just as the yellow light flashes, and break into a jog, stepping onto the curb on the other side just in time to run smack dab into a couple spilling out the front door of the Mexican restaurant on the corner.

"Sorry about that," Tristan says, pulling up short. I tug Luke's leash, drawing him closer to avoid getting the leash tangled in a familiar pair of legs.

I look up, the electricity humming across my skin fading as I lock eyes with Bear. "Oh, h-hey," I stammer. "How are you?"

"Good," he says, gaze shifting uncomfortably to his

right. "Kim and I were just grabbing some food before heading over to the concert."

I glance over to see Kim staring up at Tristan, looking anything but pleased as he offers a polite, "Hi, Kim. Nice to see you."

"Nice to see you, too," Kim says in a tone that makes it clear it's anything but nice. "You two aren't leaving so soon, are you? Things are just getting started."

"We've got some business to take care of at home." Tristan takes my hand, holding tight as he steps to the left, shifting around our exes. "But you guys enjoy it. They're a great group."

"Can't be that great if you're leaving already!" Kim lets out a high-pitched laugh, before adding in a border-line pleading voice, "Come on, Tristan, you two should stay. We can all share a bottle of wine and get caught up on the town gossip."

"Maybe some other time," Tristan tosses over his shoulder. "Have a good one."

I glance over my shoulder, lifting a hand to Bear, while deliberately avoiding eye contact with Kim. If looks could kill, hers would have already flayed my skin from my bones and tossed me head-first into a vat of acid. There was a time in my life when a look like that from Kimberly Kahn would have scared the hell out of me and sent me home shaking in my boots to spend the night wondering what fresh hell she had planned for my life.

But now, the moment I turn back to Tristan, old pain and ex-related-trauma fade away, banished in the heat and affection in his gaze. "You're sure you don't care about making them jealous anymore?"

"Nope," he says without a beat of hesitation. "Not even a little bit. What about you?"

Heart soaring, I squeeze his hand tighter. "Nope. All I care about is you, Mr. Hunter."

"Ditto, Ms. Childers." He lifts our joined palms and presses a kiss to the back of my hand. And even that simple gesture, that innocent touch, is enough to make my soul dance and my body ache.

It's definitely a night for magic, all right, and Tristan and I are on our way home to prove it.

CHAPTER 12

TRISTAN

By the time I kennel Luke, restart the U.S. Open from the very beginning to keep him company, and hurry back up the stairs—my heart pounding hard with anticipation and an unexpectedly vicious case of the jitters—Zoey is nowhere to be seen.

I move down the hall, but there's no sign of her in the bathroom or the guest room. I start toward the back of the house—assuming she must have decided to settle in the sunroom—but a sweet voice stops me, calling my name as I pass the open door to my bedroom.

I turn to see Zoey standing in the moonlight filtering through the curtains, her hair loose around her shoulders and her feet bare. And God help me, even the sight of that innocently exposed skin is enough to make me hard—instantly, painfully, desperately hard.

But that's been my default state for most of the evening. I can't remember ever wanting anything as much as I want to make love to Zoey right now. I also can't remember being this fucking nervous about getting into bed with a woman. I want so badly to make it good for her, to show her with every kiss, every touch, how much she means to me.

"I want to tell you something," she says, fingers twisting together, making me think I'm not the only one who's anxious about taking our friendship to the next level. "It's kind of embarrassing, but... Well, I want you to know."

I step inside, closing the door behind me. "Don't be embarrassed. You can tell me anything, Zoey. I'm not here to judge."

Her lips quirk at the edges. "I know you aren't, but... Well, I judge myself a little. I told myself I was focusing on work because that's what was most important to me, but that isn't really true." Her gaze drops to the floor, making her thick lashes two feathery smudges against her pale cheeks. "The truth was that I shut myself off, refusing to give anyone a chance at my heart because I..." Her breath rushes out and her fingers twist faster. "Because if I couldn't have what I really wanted, then I didn't want anything at all."

I reach up, brushing her hair gently from her face. "And what did you really want?"

She lifts her chin, her gaze crashing into mine with enough force to take my breath away. "I wanted you," she whispers, her words making me even harder, more painfully ready to show her how much I want her, too.

"Since that first week," she continues, words coming fast. "Even though you had a girlfriend and you obviously only thought of me as a friend, I couldn't help myself. And I couldn't force myself to be with anyone else. For three years, Tristan, you're the only man I've wanted to be with like this, and now it's finally happening, and I'm afraid I'm going to do something mortifying like... I don't know, like..." Her tongue slips out across her lips. "Like cry with happiness or something because I'm so—"

I cut her off with a kiss, pulling her into my arms and fusing my lips to hers, moaning as she opens for me and the sweet taste of her floods across my tongue. After a beat, her arms go around my neck, clinging tight as I back us both toward the bed.

"You can cry if you need to," I murmur against her lips as my hands roam over her curves above her clothes, pausing to squeeze her waist, her hip, and the perfect swell of her ass, forcing myself to take it slow. "I don't want you to hide anything from me, beautiful. I want you to show me everything I make you feel."

She trembles against me, shivering as I guide her back onto the bed and stretch out on top of her. "So, you don't think I'm a crazy stalker person for crushing on you for so long?"

"Does this feel like someone who thinks you're a crazy stalker person?" I rock against her thigh, letting her feel what she does to me. She gasps into my mouth and lifts into my cock, rubbing against me through my jeans, sending a lightning bolt of hunger rocketing through me in the process.

Fuck...

If it's this hot with all of our clothes still on, God only knows what it's going to feel like to be inside her.

Which means it's time for a confession of my own.

"It's been a long time for me, too." I pull back to gaze down into her face, my heart twisting at the need tightening her features. All I want to do is make this worth the wait for her, but I honestly don't know how well I'll perform the first time around. "I haven't been with anyone since the engagement ended, and I want you so fucking much, Zoey, that I'm afraid I won't last as long as I would like. But I promise I'll make it up to you if you'll give me a second shot at being the kind of lover you deserve."

Zoey threads her fingers into my hair, her eyes shining with emotion. "Don't be crazy. You're already everything I want in a lover, Tristan Hunter. Everything I want in a man. And I don't care if it lasts ten seconds or ten minutes, this is going to be so special to me. I can't wait to be with you."

Throat tight, I nod. "Me, too, Freckles."

Her lips part and heat creeps back into her expression. "Good. Then we're on the same page." She reaches for the top button of my shirt, slipping it slowly through the hole before moving to the next, eyes locked with mine. Holding her gaze, I find the zipper on the side of her dress and draw it down, pulse thundering in my ears as I pull the now loose fabric lower, confirming my suspicion that she isn't wearing a bra.

"Beautiful," I whisper, heart skipping a beat as I get my first glimpse of her breasts. Each stunning orb is far more than a handful, heavy and warm in my palms as I guide them closer together, making it easier to admire both her pale pink nipples at the same time. I bend my head, flicking my tongue across one already-tight tip and then the other before stopping to draw her left nipple deeper into my mouth, sucking and swirling until she trembles against me again.

"Oh God," she whispers, fingernails digging into my shoulders through my now-open shirt. "It's so much... So intense..."

I pull away from her addictive sweetness, already so deeply in love with her nipples I know no other pair will ever have my heart in quite the same way. "Too much?"

She shakes her head. "No, it's perfect. So good. Please, don't stop." She pushes at my shirt, guiding it off my shoulders. "Don't ever, ever stop."

I strip my sleeves down my arms and toss my shirt aside before reaching down to help her pull her dress over her head. I drop it to the floor and turn back to Zoey, breath catching at the sight of her lying there in nothing but a pair of lacy white panties. She is stunning —all softness and curves and luminous skin that glows like marble in the moonlight, so perfect it would be hard to believe she was flesh and blood if I couldn't feel her heat, smell the addictive scent of her arousal, feel her fingers warm against my skin as she unbuttons my jeans and draws the zipper down.

I bite my lip as my cock strains forward, testing the strength of my boxer briefs, but I don't move to help her. I keep my arms at my sides, watching as she drags my jeans and boxers down, baring the thick, pulsing length of my erection.

"You're so beautiful," she whispers, leaning in to

press her lips to the end of me, kissing away the fluid beading on my tip and making the entire room spin.

She kisses me again, sweeping her tongue around the pulsing head of my cock, but before she can take things any further, I fist my hand lightly in her hair, drawing her away.

"Not this time." Quickly disposing of the rest of my clothes, I shift positions, capturing her mouth with mine as I lie down beside her and tease my fingers beneath the waist of her panties. "I don't want to lose control. Not until I'm inside you."

She sucks in a breath, legs parting in a silent invitation as I glide my hand lower, beneath her panties, finding where she's so hot it makes my heart slam even faster against my ribs. "God, Zoey...you're so wet, baby."

"I want you so much," she says, cupping my cheeks in her hands as she kisses me harder, deeper. "Now. I don't want to wait any longer, Tristan. I want to be with you, to make love to you so badly."

"Me, too, more than anything," I promise as I circle her clit with my fingers, nearly losing my mind when she whimpers and bucks into my touch. She's so responsive, so sexy, that I can't stop myself from ripping her panties down her thighs and rolling back on top of her. She wraps her legs around me, bringing her molten center to press tight against my shaft, forcing me to use every last bit of willpower I have left to insist, "Wait. Condom. Let me get one from the drawer."

"I've got an IUD." Her hands skim down my back to grip my ass. "And I'm clean."

"Me, too," I say, ignoring the distant voice in my

head insisting condoms are always a must. My father ingrained in my head at an early age the importance of taking extreme precautions to prevent unwanted pregnancy. The Hunter men of past generations are famous for two things—legendary sperm counts and knocking up far more than their share of the women of Sonoma County—but right now I can't bring myself to pull away from Zoey for even a second.

And as I guide my cock to her entrance and glide slowly inside—holding her gaze as I push deep, filling her, stretching her, sinking in until I'm buried to the hilt —the thought of making a baby isn't a terrifying thought. Logically, I know we're not anywhere near ready for that kind of commitment, but on a bone-deep, soul-deep level, the thought of loving my baby into this beautiful, sexy, sweet woman feels absolutely fucking right.

So right and so hot that by the time I reach the end of her, my balls are throbbing, and bliss is pushing so hard at my self-control I know there's no time to waste.

I capture her lips for another long kiss as I bring my thumb to her clit, rubbing in slow, steady circles as I pull out and thrust back in.

"Oh, God, Tristan," she whispers, voice shaking as her nails dig into the bare skin on my shoulders. "It's even better than I imagined. It's so good. You feel so good. So perfect."

"You, too," I echo, throat tight with emotion and the heady sensations coursing beneath my skin. I expected this to be intense—it's been so long since I've been with someone, and I want Zoey like nothing else—but this is a whole new world, a wild and untamed, undiscovered country.

I've never felt anything like this overwhelming need to claim her pleasure, to make her mine, to make her come so hard she'll never want anyone buried between her thighs but me.

Mine. God, I want her to be mine. So fucking much. It's all I can do to keep from opening my mouth and letting all the things she makes me feel spill out. But I don't want to tell her I'm falling in love with her for the first time in the heat of the moment. I want to tell her when she'll know I mean every word, from my head and my heart, as well as from my cock.

God, my cock...

I'm about to go. To explode. To lose myself inside her so hard I don't know if I'll survive it, but I need her pleasure first. I increase my pressure on her clit, making her gasp and cling to me even tighter as I ride her harder, faster, holding on to my self-control by a thread.

And then, just as I'm so close to losing it I can barely breathe, she comes for me. She comes bucking and grinding into me, calling out my name as her pussy locks down around my cock. The last thread snaps.

With a cry of surrender that vibrates through my chest, I come harder than I've ever come before, my cock jerking inside her and my balls drawing tight again and again as I empty everything into her heat, her fire. My orgasm rips through me from head to toe, rearranging the universe in its wake. By the time I sag on top of Zoey—both of us breathing hard and clinging to each other as our racing hearts begin to slow—I am a changed man.

I thought I knew everything I needed to know about intimate sex. I'd assumed that spending nearly a decade with the same person, exploring every part of each other with the enthusiasm of teenagers and then the more patient love of adults, had given me a thorough education in making love.

But nothing I've experienced before can hold a candle to the bliss of being inside Zoey, to the humbling honor of knowing she's welcomed me not only into her body, but her heart. Being this close to her—so close I'm completely surrounded by her warmth and utter goodness—makes it clear I've still got so much left to learn. I didn't know it could be like this. So close. So open. So completely shameless and pure that when I brace myself on my arms to gaze down into her eyes, we communicate without saying a word.

She simply smiles, and I know that she felt it, too—that oh-so-right, oh-so-wonderful feeling.

And when I kiss her again, she tastes like everything good and safe, everything natural and right. She is the clearly marked path I've been too stupid to see through the jungle, the answer to the questions I've been too stupid to ask.

But I'm not lost or confused anymore.

I'm found, here in her arms, and as I make love to her again, I'm filled with a gratitude that takes my breath away. As I roll beneath her, letting her set the pace, I give thanks for my painful breakup and all the hellish grief that came after. It was all worth it—every second made precious because it's what it took to get me here, in bed with this woman who is as beautiful on the inside as she is on the outside.

I come again, lifting Zoey into the air as I arch my back in a desperate attempt to get closer, already knowing that I'm never going to get close enough.

CHAPTER 13

From the texts of Violet Boden
and Zoey Childers

Zoey: Violet are you awake?

Violet: Is it four thirty in the morning? Of course,
I'm awake.
Better question, why are you awake at this ungodly
hour, sweet pea? Don't tell me the insomnia monster is
after you, too.

Zoey: No. I mean, I haven't been able to sleep, but I
haven't really been trying.
Right now I'm in the kitchen eating cheesecake, but
mostly I've been lying awake, staring at the ceiling,

trying to memorize every second of the most amazing night of my life…

Violet: Well, I'm assuming you haven't won the lottery…

Zoey: That would be hard to do since I never buy tickets.

Violet: Right. And you weren't accepted as a contestant on the next season of Master Cook, Home Chefs' Edition.

Zoey: Again, hard to do, since I didn't apply.

Violet: Though, you should. You would totally win.

Zoey: Thank you, but I hate reality TV and getting yelled at, and that guy yells a lot.

Violet: He does, but not at the kids on the Little Cooks version of the show. He's actually really sweet with them. It changed the way I think about him.

Zoey: Good to know. If I make a wish on a fortune-telling carnival game and wake up back in my twelve-year-old body, thereby finding myself eligible for Little Cooks, I'll remember that.

Violet: Stranger things have happened.

Zoey: Oh, they have not! Now make a serious guess, Violet!

If I don't get to spill this news to someone soon, I'm going to explode, and you're the only person I trust who's awake at this hour. You're also my only friend who also knows the other person involved in the most amazing night of my life.

The person who made it completely, wonderfully, incomparably remarkable...

Violet: I don't have to guess, babes. I already know. You finally slept with Tristan!

Zoey: I DID! AND YOU KNOW I DON'T USUALLY KISS AND TELL, BUT THIS TIME I HAVE TO TELL BECAUSE IT BLEW MY MIND, VIOLET! MIND. IS. BLOWN!

Violet: Lol! Oh good, I'm so happy for you, babes!

Zoey: Me, too! So happy! I had no idea it could be like that, Violet!

It's been three hours since we finally agreed to stop pouncing each other and get some sleep, and I still can't feel my toes. And I know he was right and we need rest, but I don't want to sleep now, or ever again, because sex is the best thing ever!

Why didn't someone tell me it was the best?

Or that I've been doing it all wrong?!

Violet: What do you mean you've been doing it wrong? As far as I could tell, you haven't been doing it at all, honey. Unless you've been having hot hookups after hours and not telling your Aunt Vi about them.

Zoey: No, you're right, I've been a hermit lately. But my college boyfriend, Bear, and I had sex pretty much constantly for two years—indoors and outdoors, in his truck, in my car, in the shower and the rain and on a train and in a box with a fox.

Violet: I'm assuming that's a Dr. Seuss joke and not an actual sex thing I'm too old to understand, right?

Zoey: Yes, it was a joke, but the rest of it wasn't. Bear and I were insatiable, and it was great—fun and relaxed and he always made sure to you know…
Take care of me…

Violet: He made you come. You can be frank with me, honey. I've heard it all.

Zoey: Yes, he took care of that. So I thought I'd had a pretty good sex life, you know? I mean, obviously I've been in a drought for a while, but my boyfriend in high school and I had fun, and Bear and I had fun.
But none of that was anything like this…

Violet: Well, Tristan's a man, babe, not a boy. There's a difference.

Zoey: Such a difference… Just the way he looked at me was almost enough to get the job done if you know what I mean. So intense and intimate. Like he could see through me in the best way and knew exactly what I wanted, what I needed…
It was just…beautiful.
Wonderful.
Amazing and perfect and the
Best.
Banging.
Ever.

Violet: Sounds more like making love to me.
Deep feelings make a difference, too, you know.

Zoey: Oh no, Vi. I mean, I know he cares about me, but this was his first time since he and Kim broke up. He hasn't been with anyone in over a year, either! So I'm sure that had a lot to do with how epic it was for both of us.
At least, I hope it was epic for both of us…
Surely, it was epic for him, too, right? Or it wouldn't have been that way for me?
Shit, now I'm nervous…

Violet: Don't be nervous, and don't write off love so fast. You two have been good friends for a long time. Sometimes it doesn't take long to fall when you're so close to begin with. My ex and I were friends first. Chemistry entered the picture later.

Zoey: I'm not writing off love. Not for me, anyway. You know I've had feelings for him for a long time. I'm just not sure that's on his radar yet.

We ran into Kim and Bear at the square tonight…

Violet: You think he's still holding on to old feelings?

Zoey: No, not at all, but seeing her again got me to thinking about how long they were together… It just has me confused, I guess. I don't understand how someone as smart and wonderful as Tristan could be taken in by this woman.

Violet: Men can be dumb when their cocks are involved. And you don't know—his ex might have been really good at faking being a decent human being. At least when she was with him.

Zoey: I can see that, I guess. All our professors in college loved her. She could totally turn on the charm when it suited her.

Violet: Most sociopaths can, and Tristan wouldn't be the first otherwise smart and savvy guy to be taken in by one.

Zoey: She probably is a sociopath, Violet. For real. She's absolutely a horrible person. But apparently now she's pulled the wool over Bear's eyes, too. I mean, my ex isn't the brightest light on the Christmas tree, but he's a solid guy with a good heart. I can't understand what he sees in a person who spent our college career spreading rumors about me sleeping with guys for beer money and having multiple venereal diseases.

Violet: Yikes! That's awful! Does Tristan know she did that?

Zoey: No, and I don't want to tell him. If I tell him about the way she treated me, then I'll have to tell him what started it all, and I don't want to hurt him like that. If he learns she cheated on him with half the University of Sacramento, it'll break his heart all over again. Or, at the very least, make him feel like a fool.

Violet: He shouldn't feel like a fool—she should be ashamed of herself for lying and betraying his trust—but I see where you're coming from.
No need to introduce more pain into a person's life unless you absolutely have to.
Especially not when he's finally ready to fall in love again...

Zoey: Oh, stop. Don't get my hopes up.

Violet: Do it, honey. Get your hopes up. Soar on the wings of love and anticipation and enjoy every fucking minute of it. Take it from someone who's seen the best and the worst of what love has to offer—it's worth it. Even if it fades or falters, love is always worth the risk. I wouldn't take back a single minute of my life with Grant. We had an amazing fifteen years together before things went to shit, and I still treasure every second of that...

Even after being dumped for a much younger, much stupider woman, who won't stop trying to mother my teenager despite being all of nine years old than Adriana.

Zoey: Ugh. I'm sorry. So that situation hasn't gotten any better, huh?

Violet: No, but Addy is off to college next year, and she'll be able to tell all the bossy mother-figures in her life to back off and leave her alone. And Tracy means well. She's just inexperienced and has the IQ of a sea cucumber.

Zoey: Did you know that the sea cucumber can expel its internal organs and then regenerate them later? It's part of their self-defense system. They'll hurl an organ out into the water to make a predator think it got all the good, juicy stuff so it'll swim away and leave the rest of the body alone.

Violet: Like...here's my liver, go get it?

Zoey: Exactly like that. And sometimes tiny fish use the sea cucumber's anus as a sanctuary from predators. Sometimes they're mannerly about it, but sometimes they'll swim up too high and start eating the cuke's internal organs, too.

Violet: So, a sea cucumber's innards are tasty is what I'm hearing.

Zoey: I suppose so. They are featured in some Asian cuisines as well as eaten medicinally in China, so…

Violet: So, Tracey is nothing like a sea cucumber, as she is neither useful nor medicinal.

Zoey: Well, sea cucumbers also breathe through their anus—in addition to having tiny fish up in that action— so maybe there's an area of similarity there?

Violet: You know more about a sea cucumber's anus than I know about my own. Seriously. You should be on Jeopardy.

Zoey: When they decide to do an animal-trivia-only episode I'll be the first in line to apply. Right after I win Master Cook.

Violet: I'm holding you to that.
And I'm ordering you and Tristan to both call in sick today.

Zoey: Oh no, it's fine, Violet. I can go without sleep for one night and still function the next day. It's not a big deal.

Violet: It IS a big deal, and you and Tristan should take the day to sleep in and enjoy your newfound bliss. I'm already up anyway. I'll take care of the morning feeding and medicine-ing. There aren't any adoptions on the schedule today, so I'll be able to handle walk-ins until Mary and Virginia get there in the afternoon for their volunteer hours. It's fine.

Go crawl back into bed and order Tristan to take the day off.

You're his boss now, so you can totally do that.

Zoey: Probably not the best way to prove I'm boss material…

Taking a personal day my first week on the job…

Violet: Your first personal day in forever! You haven't taken a day since you were sick as a dog last spring. Go. Sleep in. Wake up and get a leisurely breakfast with your hunky new boyfriend. Enjoy the gorgeous weather.

It's supposed to be perfect today, sunny with a high of seventy-two.

I know this because I'm so old I watch the weather channel for entertainment these days. My heart can't handle much else.

Zoey: You are not old! Stop it! And the weather channel is fascinating.

Violet: Almost as good as managing my fiber intake, my

other favorite new pastime ;). Now, go get some rest girl so you can wake up refreshed and enjoy your sexy new boyfriend.

Zoey: My boyfriend...
Is it okay that I have the biggest, goofiest smile on my face right now?

Violet: It's more than okay, honey. It's perfect.

CHAPTER 14

*P*erfect…

Everything *is* perfect…

So perfect I can hardly believe this is my life.

I'm floating on air as I tiptoe back down the hall in the dark, my head so high in the clouds I nearly trip over Luke before I see him curled up on the carpet. He's camped outside my door, his new sock-toy between his paws. When he sees me, he lifts his head sharply and his tail thumps the carpet.

"Hey, buddy. How did you get out of your kennel?" I lean down, giving him a good rub behind the ears. "I'm not in there tonight. I'm sleeping in your dad's bed."

I am. I'm going back to sleep in *Tristan's* bed, where *Tristan* is currently passed out without a stitch of clothing on.

Be still my heart. And the rest of me…

Just the thought of the man who made me see stars a few hours ago is enough to fill my chest with a swarm of happy bees. God, I can't wait to be next to him again...

Luke apparently feels the same way. The devoted darling follows me down the hall to Tristan's room, whimpering softly when I duck inside, careful to keep the door closed enough to keep the sad puppy on the other side. "Sorry, baby. You know your dad doesn't like dogs in his bed."

Luke whimpers again.

"I know, I know. I'll work on him, I promise." With one last neck rub, getting deep into the fur the way Luke likes, I close the door and pad across the thick carpet to the bed.

"Work on me, huh?" Tristan asks sleepily, making me jump as I pull back the covers.

"God, you scared me," I whisper, laughing softly. "I thought you were asleep."

"I was, but then I woke up and you weren't there, and sadness consumed me." He reaches for me, drawing me into the cocoon of warmth under the blankets and against his hot, irresistible skin. "I was about to come looking for you. Make sure I hadn't scared you off."

"Why would I be scared off?" I ask, blood pumping faster as Tristan tucks me against him and I rest my cheek on his chest.

"Because I'm an insatiable sex fiend who can't get enough of your body?" His hand skims down my back to cup my bottom, building the ache already pulsing between my legs. "I'm not usually like this. You're just so...delicious."

I prop up on my arms, gazing down at him in the

dim light coming through his bedroom window. "Don't tell me you're not usually like this. I like you like this."

"Hopelessly addicted to every inch of you?" His palm glides under the waistband of the pajama pants I slipped on before heading into the kitchen for my late-night snack, his hand on my bare bottom making my breath catch.

"How do you do that?" I ask, my heart hammering as the desire building inside me surges from cool to scalding hot in seconds.

"Do what, sexy?" Tristan brushes my hair from my face, cupping my cheek as he guides my mouth closer to his.

"Make me desperate for you with just a touch?"

"You do the same thing to me." His hand slides down, over the curve of my ass, finding where I'm already so hot and wet. "God, Zoey, I love your body. I love how wet you get for me."

I whimper softly in response as his mouth claims mine, kissing me in that gentle but relentless way of his that makes me burn. His tongue strokes against mine as his fingers press inside me, making me even wetter, hotter.

"I need to taste you, beautiful," he says, his voice tight and hungry. "Can I taste you? Make you come on my mouth?"

I shiver and nod, heart skipping a beat as he rolls on top of me, deepening the kiss as he reaches for the bottom of my T-shirt. We pull apart as the fabric whooshes over my head, but then his mouth is back on mine, kissing me breathless before his lips move to my neck, taking my racing pulse with his tongue before he moves farther down.

He draws my already tight nipple into his mouth, making me cry out as electric anticipation fizzes across my skin. I arch into his tongue, moaning as he drags his teeth over my already sensitized flesh, but the last thing I want him to do is stop. I don't ever want him to stop. I want his hands, his mouth all over me. I want to be marked from head to toe with Tristan's touch, his scent. I want to drown in all the incredible things he makes me feel and never, ever come up for air.

"Fuck, Zoey, you drive me crazy." He groans as he drags my pajama pants down my legs and urges my thighs wider, revealing where I'm wet, swollen and so ready. "I can't wait to taste you."

My legs tremble as he presses a kiss to my left thigh and then my right, moving closer to the center of me. And then his tongue teases, ever so lightly, around the sensitive skin at my entrance, and I gasp. Just that touch, so feather soft, is almost enough to undo me. It isn't just the physical things he's doing to me that make my head spin. It's knowing that it's *Tristan's* mouth between my legs. *Tristan's* tongue circling my clit, *Tristan's* hands spreading my legs farther apart so he can get closer, deeper, staking his claim on my most intimate places.

I've been head over heels for this man pretty much since the moment I met him. Now, after years of being so sure I would never be anything but his friend, he's finally head over heels for me.

It's intoxicating. Exhilarating.

And after only a few minutes, I'm soaring, so close to spinning out of control that when Tristan groans against my slick skin, the vibration of his voice is enough to make me shatter.

I call his name as I come, arching into his mouth, reaching for him because I can't stand not to have my hands on him for another second. I thread my fingers through his silky-soft hair, holding on tight as he continues to pulse his tongue against me, drawing out the release until tears gather at the edges of my eyes.

I pull in a deep breath that shudders out, sending a tear slipping down the side of my face.

"Are you okay, baby?" Tristan asks as he moves back over me. "Are you crying?"

I swallow. "A little. It's just...so good."

"It is so good," he echoes in a way that leaves no doubt in my mind that he feels it too—the beautiful, crazy, amazing thrill of being so close to someone who means so much to you. He holds my gaze as he reaches between us, his eyes never leaving mine as he fits his fever-hot cock to my still pulsing entrance and glides oh-so-slowly inside.

My lips part, my soft groan of gratitude and relief mingling with Tristan's, making us both grin as he comes to a stop deep inside me.

"Did you miss me?" He guides my right leg around his hips, allowing him to sink just a tiny bit deeper, sending shockwaves through my core as he rubs against my clit. "In those three hours we were apart?"

"Yes," I whisper, wrapping my arms around him. "I missed you. So much."

"Me, too." His smile fades as he begins to move, oh-so-slowly at first, each stroke a heartbreakingly beautiful step closer to the edge, closer to him, closer to the pleasure that waits at the end of this road. "I was dreaming about you. We were outside on a blanket, and you were riding me with the sun in your hair."

"Maybe we can make that dream a reality before too long," I say, lifting into him as he glides deep again, my breath coming faster. "We're both taking a personal day today. Violet's going to hold down the fort until the volunteers arrive and close up after the kitty meet and greet."

"You're brilliant. The best boss ever." Tristan bites his bottom lip. "Just when I thought you couldn't get any hotter..." His hand slips between us, his fingers finding my clit as he begins to move faster. I moan, clinging to his shoulders as he takes me there—up, up, up to the dizzy heights I've only glimpsed with him.

I come again, gasping and fighting to keep my eyes from squeezing shut as pleasure pulses through me in sharp, aching waves. I don't want to close my eyes, I don't want to miss a second of this—of Tristan's handsome features twisting in pleasure-pain as he comes, of the way his hand shakes as he wraps his fingers around the back of my neck, pulling me in for a kiss as his cock pulses deep inside me.

I hum against his lips as the taste of us—of my sex and his mouth—teases my tongue. It's a tangy, earthy flavor that calls to something primal inside of me, something deep inside my bones that growls its approval of this man, this taste, this fire that he lights inside of me.

If we were albatrosses, I would have already picked out a nest and started the mating dance ritual. He just feels...*right*. Everything about him, from the way he drives me wild to the way he pulls me close, tucking me into the smaller spoon position and kissing my shoulder.

I sigh, so content—and exhausted—I'm on the verge of sleep in seconds. The only thing that keeps me awake is the whining at the door.

The whining that gets louder and louder the longer Tristan and I lay quietly on the bed...

"I would say that he'll eventually stop, but he's fragile on nights when he's managed to break out of his kennel." Tristan kisses my shoulder again before slipping out of bed and reaching for his jeans on the floor. "At this point, I might as well go let him outside. Before he decides we've missed morning backyard time and leaves a puddle by the door."

"I'll wait up for you," I murmur, my eyes already sliding closed again. "Hurry back."

Tristan chuckles. "Get your rest, Sleeping Beauty. I'll wake you at ten, and we'll go get waffles and French press coffee and celebrate."

"Oh yay." I smile and hum happily as I snuggle deeper into the covers. "What are we celebrating?"

"Are you kidding?" He leans over to kiss my cheek, making me smile. "Six orgasms in less than twelve hours, of course."

My brow furrows as my pleasure-overloaded and

sleep-deprived brain does the math. I force my left eye to open, "But we're on five, right?"

He grins down at me. "That's why I'm waking you up at ten. That way we'll have time for number six, with a few minutes left over to shower, get dressed, and make it to Rosewood Grocery before they stop serving breakfast at eleven."

Luke whines louder from outside, clearly not approving of this plan. I giggle as Tristan mock-glares at the door. "I hear you, Luke. Keep your pants on." Grabbing his T-shirt off the floor, Tristan turns back to me. "Don't worry. I'll leave the orgasm police outside until we're ready to leave for breakfast."

I smile, my lids heavy. "Oh, I'm not worried..."

Not worried at all...

In fact, as I slide into a deep, delicious sleep sweeter than any in recent memory, I'm completely at peace. Giddy with excitement, but peaceful at the same time. It's not a combination I've experienced before, but Tristan is rapidly redefining reality as I know it.

And I couldn't be happier about him or this brave new world...

CHAPTER 15

TRISTAN

*I*t's a morning of firsts—first morning-after, first couple's shower, first brunch, first hike to the dog park at the top of the mountain—but it feels like I've done all of this with Zoey before. Not that anything is boring or predictable, it's just all so natural, so easy. Zoey's only the second woman I've ever slept with, so I don't have much to compare this relationship to, but less than twenty-four hours in, I'm already having drastically altered feelings about my split with Kim.

Yes, it hurt like hell. And yes, I truly loved her, in the way you love people who have been in your life so long they've become a part of you. But what I had with Kim was two-dimensional compared to this. Compared to looking into Zoey's eyes and knowing she wants me for exactly who I am. Full stop.

Kim saw me, yes, but she'd made it clear from day

one that there were things that needed to change to make me worthy of continuing to be her one and only. To Kim, I was a project to be improved upon, a lump of clay with the potential to become something special if molded correctly.

With Zoey, I'm already a prize, no modifications needed.

And I feel the same way about her.

She's already perfect. From the way she giggles when she gets whipped cream on her nose after a particularly daring bite of extra thick Rosewood Grocery waffle, to the way she stops to let Luke sniff every signpost from downtown to the start of the trailhead, to the way she races him to the entrance to the dog park as soon as the familiar wrought iron gate comes into view. She is so sweet and loving and real.

And so incredibly sexy that I have to fight to keep memories from last night from my head for fear of rocking a hard-on at the dog park in front of half the little old ladies in Healdsburg.

I've always thought Zoey was pretty, and lately, "beautiful" is the word that comes to mind when I glance her way. And yes, since our first kiss, I've definitely been attracted to her, but I never expected it to be so white hot between us.

In her day-to-day life, Zoey's a relatively reserved person. She's poised and classy, the kind of woman you could easily imagine running for office and not having to worry about any skeletons in her closet.

In my secret, not-safe-for-work thoughts, I'd

assumed she would probably carry that restraint into the bedroom. Not that she wouldn't be passionate or sexy, but that she might be the kind of person who finds it hard to let go.

But that's not the case. Not even a little bit.

She's wild. Shameless. Mind-blowingly sexy, and so uninhibited I have no doubt that we're soon going to find ourselves in previously unexplored territory. At least for me. I want to do everything with her, memorize every inch of her gorgeous body, learn everything that gives her pleasure and makes her come for me, calling out my name in that way that makes me crazy.

Shit...

And now I'm hard. Again. For the tenth time this morning.

Willing the man downstairs to calm the fuck down, I take a deep breath and bend low, grabbing the stick from Luke as he bounds back across the grass from the other end of the park.

"You ready for a big one?" I ask, the words making Luke's tail work harder. "All right, here it comes." I draw back my arm and hurl the stick as hard as I can, sending it arcing up into the air, where it hovers for a moment in the blue, blue sky before tumbling back to earth to land just barely within the boundaries of the iron fence.

"Nice one," Zoey says, nudging my hip with hers as she takes a sip of her coffee.

"Thanks." I wrap an arm around her waist, loving the feel of her so close. "This isn't my first time at the dog park. I've had time to perfect my form."

"You really do have perfect form." She glances up at

me, her pink lips curving wickedly. "I would give you an A plus for form, in fact."

I nod, fighting the urge to kiss the grin off her pretty face. "Oh yeah? And how about endurance?"

She wrinkles her nose and bobs her head side to side. "Pretty good. A solid B minus."

My brows shoot up. "B minus? I was going strong until two a.m., slept a couple hours—not much more than a nap, really—and was ready to go again as soon as you got back in bed at four thirty. How is that a B minus, Childers?"

"I'm not saying it wasn't good," she says with a shrug. "I'm just saying there's still room for improvement. I, for example, didn't sleep at all until four-thirty."

"Because you're a vampire," I say. "Clearly. And that's an unfair advantage."

She laughs. "I'm not a vampire. I usually go to bed no later than ten. Last night I was just…keyed up."

I draw her fully into my arms as I bend my face closer to hers. "I like you keyed up. I would like to get you keyed up again in the very near future, in fact."

Zoey links her wrists behind my neck. "Surely we can't keep this up, can we? It's not natural. We're going to injure ourselves."

"I don't injure easily, and it feels perfectly natural to me." I smooth one hand down to rest on the curve of her ass. "I can't remember anything that's felt more natural than being inside you."

Her cheeks go instantly red as her eyes dart quickly to the left. "Stop. Someone will hear you."

"No, they won't," I murmur. "I'm whispering."

"And I'm sure I'm turning bright red."

"I like you bright red," I say, pulling her closer as I dip my head to kiss her neck. I'm about to describe all the ways I would like to get her even redder when my cell dings loudly in my pocket. I curse softly, making Zoey laugh as she pulls away.

"Whew. Saved by the bell. Is it Deacon with a cow watch update again?"

I frown hard at the unexpected text. "No, it's Kim. She says we need to talk. To *urgently talk* is her exact phrase."

Zoey's brow furrows. "That's strange…"

"It is," I say, turning the ringer off before slipping my phone into my back pocket with a shrug. "But I don't see how we could have anything urgent to discuss, and I refuse to let her rain on this day. This is our day, and it's all sunshine, baby."

"It is," Zoey says, but a frown still knits her forehead.

"What's wrong?" I ask, resting a hand on the small of her back because I can't resist the urge to touch her for more than a minute or two.

She shakes her head. "Nothing, I just… I don't know. It's hard for me to imagine you with her. You're so kind, and she's so…difficult."

"She can be difficult," I agree. "But I grew up with difficult. My mom was always fighting with my dad, and when he wasn't fighting with my mom, Dad was fighting with his other women of the moment. Deacon and his ex-wife were a match made in hell, and Rafe and Dylan were either best friends or fight-to-the-death mortal

144

enemies—depending on the day and if one of them had forgotten to eat breakfast. Compared to all that, Kim was relatively calm." I lift a shoulder and let it fall. "And I was young when we met. By the time I realized how much work Kim was, we'd been together for three years and infatuation had become something more. And she did make me feel loved and important. I liked that."

Zoey nods. "Who wouldn't? Feeling loved and important is good."

"But it was never anything like this, like last night," I find myself confessing, though I should probably keep my mouth shut until we've been together longer. But I don't want to hide the way she makes me feel, and I'm not sure I could if I tried. "This feels...special."

Her face breaks into a smile so bright I swear I can feel it warm against my skin.

"Does the smile mean you agree?" I ask.

With a giggle she throws her arms around me, hugging me tight. "Yes! I agree. You don't know how happy it makes me to hear you say that."

"I'm getting an idea." I wrap my arms around her with a grin, ignoring the repeated buzzing in my pocket. Kim doesn't like being ignored, but what Kim likes or doesn't like isn't my problem anymore.

I don't have any problems at the moment, in fact, except maybe how quickly I can invent a stick-throwing machine, so I don't have to stop touching Zoey for even a few seconds at a time.

I mention this idea to Zoey after throwing another doozy for Luke, and she agrees that it's solid. "Or we could learn to kiss and throw sticks at the same time," she teases. "Take our multi-tasking to the next level."

"You're brilliant." I kiss her again as my ass continues to vibrate. I make a mental note to block Kim's number, and then I'm so caught up in Zoey's kiss, her touch, her sweetness that there's no room for anyone in my thoughts but her.

CHAPTER 16

Halloween

$\mathcal{I}$'m awoken from my perfectly lovely dream featuring Tristan skinny-dipping in my favorite swimming hole by slugs squirming through my bare toes—hot, squishy, slobbery slugs.

I bolt into a seated position, a scream clawing up my throat only for it to end in a yip of surprise when I see Luke grinning at me from the end of the bed. Somehow, he's managed to pull up the comforter, pull off my socks, and—judging from the amount of slobber surrounding my feet and dampening the sheets—has apparently been licking my toes for quite some time.

"Oh, man, Luke." I scrunch my nose. "This is getting weird, buddy."

"At least he didn't eat your socks this time," Tristan says sleepily. "They're down there on the floor. I call that progress."

"I call it gross," I mutter.

"It's not gross." Tristan's hand slips up the back of my sleep shirt, cool against my sleep warm skin. "You're very lickable."

"Ditto." I grin at him over my shoulder, smile widening as I see that his hair is sticking up on one side and completely flat on the other. Call me crazy, but I love seeing him sleep-mussed and imperfect. It makes me feel special, to be one of the only people in the world who knows what Tristan looks like before he's completed his meticulous grooming rituals. "So why isn't Luke hot after your sexy man toes?"

Tristan rolls his eyes with a soft sigh. "Who among us can explain the mysteries of the heart, dear Zoey? It wants what it wants, and Luke's heart clearly has a thing for your foot stink and yours alone."

I reach out, slapping his leg beneath the covers. "I do not have stinky feet! At least I didn't when I went to bed, before they were bathed in slobber."

"I will remind you that you're the one who lobbied for the dog in the bed. I was quite happy tucking Luke into his kennel downstairs with some tennis to send him off to dreamland."

"But he got lonely down there." I sigh as Luke leans in to sniff my ankle, then decides to give it a few kisses while he's at it. "All right, that's enough, psycho. Keep your tongue to yourself, or your dad is going to bring me around to his way of thinking and it'll be back to the basement for you." I shoo Luke off the bed as I reach for my robe on the chair in the corner. "Go on. Meet me at the door, and I'll let you outside."

At the magic word—*outside*—Luke lets out a happy bark and bounds joyfully from the room, ready for another morning of christening the grass and terrorizing the garden slugs.

"I'll get the coffee started, baby," Tristan says. "You want oatmeal, too?"

I pause, leaning against the doorway, taking a moment to soak in the everyday wonderful of waking up with my favorite person, of having him call me baby, of knowing I'll come back from collecting the morning dog doo and breakfast and coffee will be waiting for me because my boyfriend loves feeding me and ensuring I'm caffeinated.

It's enough to make a girl hope the hardware store's door delivery gets delayed another week, and another, and another...

"Yes, please," I say, my heart filling as I watch Tristan sit up, the early morning sun catching the hair on his arms and making it shine. God, he's beautiful. And mine. It still blows my mind. "Oatmeal sounds great."

His lips curve into a crooked grin. "How do you make the word oatmeal sound so sexy?"

"Practice," I say, with a wink, making him laugh. "See you in ten for that oatmeal date, mister."

"I'll have it waiting, gorgeous."

His laughter follows me down the hall and into the sunroom, where Luke is waiting by the door, his tail wagging fast.

"Okay, but no eating the slugs this time, you could catch something," I say as I unlock the deadbolt and let him out, stepping into the only slightly cool morning air. It's been such a long, toasty autumn, but Indian Summer can't last much longer.

Halloween is tonight, for goodness sake.

Stepping into the sandals I've taken to leaving on the stoop, I grab a biodegradable bag from the box on the shelves near the door and follow Luke out into the damp grass. It's another perfectly lovely morning, like every morning I've woken up in this house, with this man, in this new version of my life that is so exactly what I dreamed about that a part of me still worries it will vanish in the next blink and I'll wake up alone in my little apartment.

If it weren't for our God-awful neighbors, Tristan and I would be floating through the world in our own rosy, dreamy, couple bubble. But between Kim's daily texts to Tristan, insisting they have a private meeting to discuss mysterious "important" things she needs to communicate, and Bear's early morning "accidental" meetings with me, Kim and Bear are doing their best to intrude upon our world built for two.

As if summoned by my thoughts, Bear's deep voice calls out cheerily from the other side of the fence, "Hey, there, neighbor! Happy Halloween."

"Happy Halloween." I force a smile as Luke gambols around the yard, taking his sweet time doing his business, and run a hand through my sleep-rumpled hair.

If Bear were the type to notice bedhead, I would feel self-conscious. But he's always been oblivious to things like that, as well as to non-verbal cues that a girl would enjoy a little more space and a little less neighborly interaction with her ex-boyfriend.

"Are you and Tristan going to the party at the Raven tonight?" Bear plucks an orange from the tree, though surely he must have enough oranges to start his own farm-to-table juice stand by this point. "Sounds like it's going to be good times. Live band, then a DJ. Open bar and mandatory costumes for all."

"We don't have any set plans that I know of," I lie, not wanting to risk our Halloween agenda getting back to Kim.

I have no idea if Bear realizes that Kim has been texting her ex at least once or twice a day, but he clearly seems eager to reestablish some sort of relationship between the two of us. I can't tell if he just wants to be friends or something more—Bear is a hard read for things like that—but, either way, I wish he would give me some space. I'll always have fond memories of our time together, but I'd like to focus on the future right now, not the past.

"You should check it out then," he says. "I think there are still tickets available and I know you love an excuse to get dressed up. Remember that zombie cheerleader costume from sophomore year? That was awesome. You rocked that one hard."

"Thanks," I say, silently willing Luke to get down to business so I can go inside and grab a lightning-fast shower and a leisurely breakfast—in that order. "I do have a costume," I confess as Bear lingers on his ladder, though by now his basket is almost full. "I'm going as Ursula from *The Little Mermaid* and Luke is going to be my evil minion, the electric eel."

Bear laughs. "Sweet! I always thought she was kind

of hot, you know? I mean, call me crazy, but a purple lady in a skin-tight leather outfit with tentacles..." He waggles his bushy brows. "Sign me up."

I nod awkwardly, not sure how to respond, but thankfully Luke saves the day by assuming the squat position.

"All right then, have a good one. Hope we see you around," Bear says, his upper lip curling ever-so-slightly as he backs down the ladder, confirming my suspicion that he's grossed-out by dog poo.

Which is hysterical in a guy who positions himself as an extreme adventurer, mountain man kind of person. Surely he's faced down more formidable sights than a golden retriever taking a discreet crap in his own yard?

"Have a good one," I echo as Bear disappears. I cross to the corner of the yard, collect Luke's offering, and am about to hurry back inside when hushed whispers on the other side of the fence catch my attention.

Brow furrowed, I lean closer, ears straining, but I can only make out a few words. Bear whispering "patience" and then a feminine voice muttering something about "running out of time" in a frustrated tone. I'm not one-hundred percent sure, but that second voice sounds a heck of a lot like Kim's...

What in the world could she be running out of time for?

She and Bear are living happily ever after and headed back to the land Down Under after the New Year... Right?

So why is she out here lurking in the bushes on the other side of the fence, waiting to have a whispered chat with Bear as soon as he's done sticking his unwanted nose into my morning?

It's all smells very, *very* fishy. So fishy, in fact, that my stomach feels unsettled for reasons that have nothing to do with my spitty dog toes or scooping doggie doo. I haven't been caught in the crosshairs of Kim's agenda for years, but I remember how miserable it is to be swept up in her drama. I want *no* part of that. I just want to enjoy my time with Tristan, relish every second of falling in love with him, and ignore the outside world.

But experience has taught me to ignore Kim at my own peril.

I ponder the problem as I shower, but by the time I've washed away the dog spit and dressed in jeans, a red tee, and a matching gingham-checkered shirt that the new parrot rescue seems to find comforting, I'm no closer to an answer. But I do know this—I don't want to worry Tristan until I know more. Kim's already driving him crazy with her too-flirty-for-just-friends texts. I don't want to put more irritation on his plate unless I have a better idea of what's going on.

More importantly, I don't want to help Kim occupy any more of his headspace. I prefer to be the one dominating that arena—thank you very much.

"Berries and jam or honey and nuts?" Tristan asks as I breeze into the kitchen. "Take your pick; I put both by your bowl. And do you want a three cheese sandwich or tofu salad and arugula on wheat for lunch? My treat, and I'm packing."

"You certainly are." I stop behind him, wrapping my

arms around his waist as he pulls the bread out of the cabinet. "Have I told you how much I'm enjoying our sleepovers, lately?"

He turns to me, pulling me closer. "Maybe, but I'd love to hear it again." His brow knits. "Or maybe it would be better if you show me…"

I lean into him with a smile, relishing the feel of his body pressed close to mine. "We only have twenty minutes before we have to leave for work."

"Plenty of time, assuming you don't mind eating your oatmeal on the road."

"Road oatmeal works," I say, moaning into his mouth as he bends low, capturing my lips for a long, lingering kiss. "But I don't want to interrupt your sandwich making."

"Fuck sandwich making," he says, picking me up, making me giggle as I wrap my legs around his waist.

"No, fuck me, please," I murmur as he carries me back toward the bedroom.

"You don't have to ask me twice," he says, eyes darkening. And then he shuts the door and proves he's a man of his word, banishing every worry from my mind.

CHAPTER 17

*A*nimals get every bit as excited—and freaked out—around the holidays as people do. Maybe they can feel the excitement building in their human caretakers as the leaves start to change and a new year approaches. Or maybe it's something instinctual tied to cooling temperatures. But the madness usually starts around Halloween and continues through the end of January, when the sun finally starts to return.

This year is no different.

Zoey and I arrive at the shelter to find the dogs howling at a raccoon that somehow broke into the kennel and is reaching through the bars to steal the dog food left on the floor after last night's feeding. The cats in the kennel next door are agitated by the dogs' racket, and our new parrot resident is out of his cage and stalking back and forth on the ceiling beam above the office, sneezing repeatedly.

"Keep Luke here. I'll get rid of the raccoon," I say as Zoey grabs Luke's collar and holds on tight.

"Be careful!" she calls after me. "The raccoons around here are mean as spit."

"I know, I will," I assure her, touched by the worry in her voice. But I grew up on a farm and have more than my share of experience with cranky raccoons.

Grabbing the broom from the supply closet, I shoo the hissing and spitting creature back out into the woods behind the shelter, soothe and feed the dogs, and let them and Luke out into the fenced-in dog run for some exercise. On my way to do the same soothe-and-feed routine for the cats, I swing into the office to see Zoey standing on her desk, her outstretched hand filled with what looks like chunks of banana as she coos at the parrot now swaggering around in circles on the light fixture.

"Looks like you're getting closer," I say softly. The parrot sneezes violently in quick succession in response, and I cross my arms over my chest with a sigh. "I guess I need to call the vet in Santa Rosa, the one who specializes in birds. Dr. Prest couldn't find anything wrong with the Captain yesterday, but if he's still sneezing this much, we should probably get a second opinion."

"Maybe not." Zoey lifts her hand higher, closer to the skittish bird. "I was doing some reading yesterday while you were out cleaning the pens. Turns out parrots imitate a lot of their primary human's behavior, not just words or phrases. And the reason Captain's owner had to give him up was that she found out she was allergic to the dander in his feathers. Allergies can lead to a lot of sneezing, so…"

I hum appreciatively as the dots connect. "He's not sick; he's just being a parrot. You should be a pet detective."

Zoey glances over her shoulder, eyes sparkling as she laughs. "Oh my God, I loathe that movie. It's so unspeakably awful in every way."

"That's why they should remake it as a documentary, starring you, the savvy animal-whispering pet detective who gets behind the sneeze," I tease.

"Well, so far I'm not getting far with the Captain with my whispers. Or my banana," she says, lowering her arm with a sigh. "You have any other ideas? Because I really don't want to be walking back and forth underneath him all day, waiting for the bomb to drop, so to speak."

I chew the inside of my cheek, trying to remember if there was anything pertinent in the Captain's file that might lead to his recapture, but the details are fuzzy. "Let me grab his folder and see if I can find anything that might help—maybe a favorite food or something."

"Perfect. In the meantime, I'll go feed and comfort the cats." Zoey pops the banana chunks into her mouth, brushes her palm on her delicious, jean-clad bottom, and then hops down off the desk. She's clearly on a mission, but as she passes by, I can't help wrapping an arm around her waist and leaning down to steal a quick kiss.

"What was that for?" she asks, grinning against my lips.

"Nothing, just happy you're here."

Her smile widens. "I'm happy you're here, too."

"Loose lips sink ships!" the Captain screeches from overhead, making Zoey and I laugh. "Loose lips sink ships!"

"That one's just full of surprises," she says, patting my chest. "Good luck."

I head into my old office to flip through the stack of files in the inbox on the edge of Zoey's desk—the ones Violet hasn't gotten around to scanning into our database just yet. I find the Captain's, but before I can flip it open my phone vibrates in my back pocket. I tug it out to see a text from Deacon—*Cow Watch Daily Update: Dad thinks she's getting close and wants to make sure you're keeping your phone handy. He won't admit it, but I can tell he's nervous about handling the birth without you here.*

Brow furrowing, I text back—*Why? I mean, I know it's been a while since we had livestock on the property, but Dad helped birth calves all the time when we were growing up.*

A beat later, Deacon responds—*Not twins. And those were working cows, not a pet like Moo-donna. The Old Man's gone soft on her, bro. I swear, he's nearly as worried as he was when Emma went into labor.*

I grin. *Gotcha. Well, let the old softie know I plan on being there for the birth—no matter what time of day or night. Which reminds me, what time are you getting to the party tonight?*

Deacon assures me he'll be at the costume party at our family friend's house at seven on the dot, in time to catch the trick-or-treating action in the neighborhood. *I asked the twins to come, too, but they're hitting a haunted house in Rohnert Park and going to a bonfire at a friend's house later. They're too busy to hang out with their lame old man.*

I sink into the armchair in the corner of the office with the file in my lap, wondering if I should call Deacon and assure him with something more personal than a text that the boys are thrilled to have him home. But before I can decide, my brother shoots over—*Gotta run. Dylan needs me to help take a load of pumpkins over to the community center. See you tonight.*

I send him a thumbs-up and dig into the file, comforted by the fact that Deacon is going to be spending the morning with Dylan. Dylan has his cranky moments, but beneath his tough-guy act, he's got a damned good heart. He'll cheer Deacon up and keep our oldest brother from feeling bummed by empty nest syndrome.

"Find anything?" Zoey appears in the doorway, a fluffy white Persian in her arms.

"Not yet. I got sidetracked by the daily cow watch text." I lift my gaze from the folder, arching a pointed brow at Honey-Mew-Mew. "Are you sure that's a good idea? One look at that killer feline and the Captain might never come down."

Zoey hums beneath her breath. "True, but poor Honey was so stressed out she was about to lick her own tail off. She told me she needed dedicated snuggle time and maybe some tuna from my apartment."

Her apartment...

I don't like that combination of words, but despite hardware store incompetence and repeatedly delayed deliveries from their supplier, her door will eventually be fixed. And then she'll move out of my house and out of my bed, only to return for the occasional date night sleepover.

The thought is…vile.

Zoey laughs. "Are you okay?"

"Fine," I say, flipping the file closed.

"You looked like you just swallowed something awful."

I force a smile. "Worse, I figured out how we're going to get Captain off the light fixture. It involves dancing."

Zoey snorts. "You're kidding me."

"I'm not. His previous owner said he loves nothing more than a disco groove session followed by raisins and a nap."

"Oh my. Disco…" Zoey grins wickedly. "I can't wait to see this, baby. I know how much you love to fast dance."

I shoot a mock-glare her way and point to where her purse slouches on her desk. "Pull up *Saturday Night Fever*. I know you've got the soundtrack."

Zoey giggles. "I do! And I'm not even a bit ashamed of it. Disco music is happy music. Let me put Honey in the playroom, and I'll be right back."

"You're not watching me fast dance," I call after her as she scurries away.

"Oh, yes, I am," she calls back. "And I'm going to film it for the shelter social media page! Show Sonoma County how far we're willing to go to help our animals!"

"Not happening, Childers. Not a chance," I insist, but I know I won't be able to say no to her. I lift my gaze to the Captain. "Come on, buddy. Come down and spare us both the dance party, okay?"

"Dancing Queen," the parrot crows, clearly not on my side. "Dancing Queen!"

"Excellent choice, Captain. And I just happen to have it on one of my playlists." Zoey claps her hands as she hurries back into the room, practically bouncing with excitement. "Now, this is the way to start a Friday!" Wagging her fingers up and down in what I vaguely recognize as a disco move from a movie I watched years ago, Zoey shimmies over to her purse and grabs her phone.

And God help me, though I hate any kind of dancing but slow-dancing like Luke hates being separated from Zoey's socks, her excitement is contagious. By the first trill of the piano keys, I'm grinning. And by the time the singers begin cooing about "digging the dancing queen," I'm out on the dance floor—the empty space between the desk and Luke's bed—getting my groove on.

"That's right, you've got it!" Zoey shouts encouragement as I mimic her moves—more finger-wagging and pointing with some spinning mixed in.

Soon, the Captain is bobbing his head in time to the beat and bouncing from side to side, so clearly swept up in the magic of disco that I forget to be self-conscious. I'm an average fast dancer on my best days, and this is the first time I've ever boogied to ABBA, but with Zoey grinning and spinning beside me and a happy animal croaking his joy as he hops down from the light to dance on the desk, I finally get it.

Disco can be a blast...as long as you're in the right company.

But I think I'd enjoy watching paint dry with Zoey.

As I spin her under my arm, gazing down into her blissed-out face, I'm struck by a rush of emotion so intense it's like a wave knocking me off my feet. It hits hard and fast—shocking, but at the same time somehow so expected.

I'm already in love with her, not simply on my way there.

I'm in love with Zoey, and it isn't something that happened all of a sudden. This has been building for months, maybe even years.

Maybe even before Kim and I called it quits...

Looking back over the past few years, all my best memories have Zoey in them. She's been my partner, my co-conspirator, and the person I turn to when I need to talk to someone who knows how to listen with her whole heart. And yes, she's right—I could stand to open up more—but for a man raised in a house full of Let's-Not-Talk-About-Feelings alpha males, I already share more of my vulnerable underbelly than any of my brothers.

And I share that part of myself with her. Not with Kim. Not with Dad, Deacon, Dylan, or Rafe. Not with my friends in town or my buddies from high school or any of the very nice shelter volunteers with whom I've formed close connections in the past few years.

Zoey is my touchstone, my home base, the person I

trust for advice that comes from a good heart and a level head. And I know she feels the same way about me. We fit together on a molecular level, in that soul-deep way I'd deluded myself into thinking Kim and I would find if I just stayed the course and kept trying to get better, stronger, more successful and perfect in her eyes.

But Kim and I never would have made it for the long haul. We were every bit as mismatched as Zoey and I are a perfect fit.

So really, the amazing thing isn't that I'm madly in love with her. The crazy thing is how long it took me to see the truth right in front of my face.

Honestly, it scares the shit out of me.

I've always thought I could trust my gut and intuition. I'm the person my brothers have come to for advice, ever since we were kids, and I've always felt I could be trusted to offer grounded, realistic solutions.

But this whole time I've been so fucking blind...

As "Dancing Queen" ends and something from *Saturday Night Fever* begins to play, Zoey reaches out to squeeze my hand. "You want to grab him? Or you want me to give it a go?"

For a second, I'm confused—so lost in thought I'm not sure what she's talking about—but then she glances at the parrot happily grooving on the desk, and it all becomes clear. So clear that I don't hesitate to say, "Let's dance some more."

Her eyes widen. "You're kidding."

I shake my head, absolutely certain. "I'm not. He's having a blast, I'm having a blast, he's not sneezing anymore..."

"It's a win, win, win." Zoey lifts her arms and links her wrists behind my neck with a fond smile. "I like this fast-dancing side of you. And you're really not bad at it, you know."

"And you're the sweetest liar, I know." I kiss her as we sway in a circle, loving the way her laughter tastes on my lips.

So I've been asleep.

So what?

I'm awake now. The blinders are off, and the way forward is clear, and I'm going to make my first move as a clear-headed man in love tonight.

CHAPTER 18

TRISTAN

*A*fter a chaotic morning, things mellow out as the day moves forward. The Captain hops back into his cage with a spring in his step, the dogs enjoy naps in the shade in between pre-adoption meetings with prospective humans, the more feral cats tolerate a low-key socializing session with Violet and Zoey, and I make plans.

Plans as I clean out the stables.

Plans as I draw up an order for a gravel delivery for the parking lot.

Plans as Zoey hitches a ride home with Violet—needing extra time to get into full Ursula costume—and I promise to be home as soon as I finish the final evening feeding and get the office ready for our faithful volunteers to run the show this weekend.

I'm flying pretty high—anxious, but certain I don't want to wait another second to tell Zoey the way I feel

—when the arrival of a last-minute visitor sends storm clouds surging in.

Of all the days for Kim to decide to show up for an unexpected visit...

What the hell is she doing here, anyway?

Cursing softly beneath my breath, and steeling myself for a run-in with my ex, I lift a hand as she approaches the counter, tugging my earbuds out with the other. "Hey, I was just doing a last clean up around the office. We're closing in ten minutes."

Kim smiles thinly, her shoulders hunching as she rests her arms on the reception counter. "I know. I waited until the end of the day on purpose. I was hoping we could talk... If you're not too busy."

Jaw clenching, I nod as I tuck the push vacuum into its corner behind Luke's bed. I'd rather get out of here ASAP, but maybe this talk will mean an end to the daily texting. "Sure. Just let me grab Luke from the dog run. We can talk on the way to the car."

"I'd rather it be just the two of us, actually," she says, making me stop in the hallway, turning back to face her as she adds, "I get kind of sad when I see him, you know? I've really missed him since I've been away."

Sliding my hands into my jeans pockets, I amble back toward the counter. "He missed you, too. After you left, the eating Zoey's socks thing got so much worse. For a while there, I thought I was going to have to put a muzzle on him to keep him out of surgery."

Kim's forehead bunches in concern. "Oh, man, the poor guy. I'm sure he must have been so confused." She pauses, lacing and unlacing her fingers as she sighs. "I'm sure you must have been confused, too."

I shake my head. "I don't want to do this, Kim. That's why I haven't been responding to your texts. Maybe nine months ago, even six months ago, this could have been helpful, but now..." I lift my shoulders and let them fall. "It's over. It's in the past, and I think that's where it should stay. We had a good run, things ended, and now we can both move on."

"But not as friends," she says, her eyes beginning to shine. "You don't want to be friends, do you? No matter how cool I'm trying to be about Zoey?"

Head rearing back, I blink. "Excuse me? Why wouldn't you be cool about Zoey?"

"Come on, Tristan," Kim says, her voice taking on that sugar-frosted edge that used to soften me up, even in the middle of a fight. "You know why. Surely she's told you at least some version of what happened between us in college."

I hesitate, not wanting to admit that Zoey hasn't told me much. Being kept in the dark by my pretend fiancée won't play well right now. Worse, it would give Kim another thing to pick at before she gets around to whatever really brought her here in the first place.

So I cross my arms, deliberately keeping my response vague. "She has. What about it?"

"Well, you're a smart guy. You know that every story has two sides." Kim circles slowly around the counter to stand in the doorway leading into the office.

She's wearing a nearly transparent pale blue skirt I used to love and a white linen shirt unbuttoned far enough to show the considerable cleavage above her camisole, but she does nothing for me. Less than nothing. I actually find the sight of her vaguely repulsive and wish she wasn't blocking the swiftest route to my car.

I'm finally completely free of her. Free...

It's enough to make my heart lift, even with Kim still standing there with a stubborn set to her jaw, clearly determined to drag me back into her orbit. But she's out of luck this time. I am beyond her reach, so over her I'll never have to worry about Kim so much as bruising my heart again, let alone breaking it.

"Yes, I said some tough things to Zoey." Kim presses her lips together as she shakes her head. "But after all the lies she told about me, I couldn't help myself. Seriously, she made up so many crazy stories, Tristan. Just... insane stuff." She blinks, lifting her gaze to the ceiling. "At first, I thought she was just jealous and was willing to do absolutely anything to get attention. But then I started to worry that it might be something...more serious."

I study Kim's face, fighting the urge to tell her to go shovel her shit somewhere else because no one here is buying, but a part of me is curious as to what's behind this smear attempt. Does she just want to make sure I never find happiness with someone else? Or is there something else on her agenda?

Surely she can't think there's a snowflake's chance in hell of the two of us getting back together?

"Get to the point, Kim," I say, instead of the several, harsher things floating through my head. "I assume there is a point?"

Kim presses her hands together in front of her. "Please, don't be mad. I promise I'm not trying to screw things up for you. If you're happy with Zoey, then I'm happy for you. I'm just worried and want to make sure you're safe."

My eyebrows shoot up. "Safe from who? Zoey?"

"That's why I've been texting so often," Kim says, the skin around her eyes tightening with worry. "Just to make sure everything is still good with you two. I mean, after the way she stalked me in college, I wouldn't put physical violence past her. Especially if she thought that it would hurt me in some way. I can tell she doesn't like that I'm with her ex. She's been coming over every morning and driving Bear crazy, spying on him through the fence while he's working in the garden and asking all kinds of personal questions about us."

I hold up both hands, shaking my head. "What are you even talking about, Kim? Seriously, you sound like a crazy person right now."

Kim's hands fall helplessly to her sides. "I know! I'm sorry. But when you're talking about crazy people, sometimes *you* end up sounding crazy. But I swear to you, Zoey's acting weird again, the way she did in college. All...obsessed with me and weird, and honestly, if I'd realized Zoey from college was also your friend Zoey from work, I would have warned you about her years ago, Tristan. Immediately." She shakes her head with a sigh. "I would have probably encouraged you to fire her. Yes, she may have changed and gotten psychological help or whatever, but I went through too much with that girl to trust her with anyone I care about."

My breath rushes out as tension digs into my face. I want to shut this down, but I have no idea what to say to Kim right now. It's all so wild. I have no idea how to connect her story with the Zoey I know.

But then, I also don't know anything about what happened between Kim and Zoey in college, because Zoey refuses to tell me.

"Because I still care about you." Kim takes one slow step closer and then another. "I know I did a shit job of showing it, but... I was scared, Tris. I was only twenty-five. I didn't feel ready to walk down the aisle. I had to prove to myself that I could make it on my own first. If I hadn't, I never would have had the faith in myself that I have now. I would have always worried that I'd be helpless without you, and that's no way to build a strong marriage."

Driving a clawed hand through my hair, I close my eyes, suddenly so fucking tired.

I don't want to wander down memory lane with Kim. I don't want to rehash the details of our break-up or remind her of the cruel way she ended things. I just want to go home, take a power nap, and wake up and forget this conversation ever happened.

"I have to go, Kim," I say, sniffing as I open my eyes. "I can't unpack all this right now. Maybe ever. Nothing you're saying makes sense to me, and I can't go back. Neither of us can."

"People say that," Kim whispers, tears filling her eyes. "But it's not true. Sometimes the only way forward is back. That's why I'm here Tristan. I can't move on with Bear or anyone else until I know you're okay.

You're the most important person in my life...even if you're not in my life anymore."

"I'm okay," I say, my throat tight. "I'm better than okay, actually."

"Are you really, though?" she asks, her throat working. "If you don't even know the woman you're about to marry?"

"I know Zoey." I narrow my gaze, hoping Kim can see how close I am to asking her to leave. "And this conversation is over. Move on, Kim. Be happy. Let us both let go of the past."

After a long moment, she nods, her gaze dropping to the floor. "Okay. I'm sorry if I upset you. Truly, all I want is to make sure you stay safe." She shifts back a step, breath hitching. "And to tell you I'm sorry for hurting you. If there's one thing I could take back in my entire life, that would be it."

Before I can respond, Kim turns and hurries out of the office, across the deserted waiting room, and through the front door into the rosy evening sunlight.

I watch her go, unable to name the feelings rushing through my chest. I suppose I should feel vindicated—she clearly regrets the shitty way she broke things off. Or maybe I should be experiencing a heaping helping of grim satisfaction—she broke my heart, but it looks like her heart didn't escape unscathed. Or maybe I should simply be relieved that it's finally over. She said her piece, I listened, and we agreed to disagree before amicably parting ways.

But all I feel as she gets into her car and drives away is...confused.

And sad.

And angry that Kim's put a damper on the fun of the day.

But then, her visit hasn't changed anything, really. I still trust Zoey, I still care about Zoey, and I'm still planning to tell her how much she means to me. Tonight. As soon as I put the finishing touches on my plan.

Thoughts shifting back to my romance to-do list, I fetch Luke and head out, locking the door behind me. By the time Luke and I reach the hardware store—mere minutes before they close—I've put Kim mostly out of my mind. I'll talk through what happened with Zoey when I get home, and then we'll move on to bigger and better things—like turning another aspect of our pretend into sweet, sweet reality.

CHAPTER 19

ZOEY

*Y*ou know you've reached a special place in a friendship when you find yourself standing in your shower wearing nothing but a bandeau bikini top and a pair of black spandex shorts, while your girlfriend paints you from hairline to cleavage in purple body spray.

The thought makes me want to laugh, but I keep my eyes closed and my breath held, having learned the hard way about the unpleasantness of inhaling body paint.

"One more second," Violet says, moving the misting wand over my shoulders. "Lift your ponytail. You don't want purple hair."

I oblige, and a moment later, Violet shouts, "Done!" and flicks off the motor on the spray kit. "But don't move," she adds. "Give yourself a few seconds to dry first."

"Thank you for this," I say, eyes slowly blinking open

as the sticky feeling on my lids fades. "Truly, it goes on so much smoother with help."

"My pleasure." Violet crosses her arms, studying me with a bemused smile. "Though I think you're the only woman in the world who thinks Halloween is a good time to paint herself the color of an eggplant and slap on a gray wig."

"A white wig," I correct.

"Oh, so more of an eighty-year-old woman than a sixty-year-old one? Be still my heart... How will poor Tristan ever control himself?"

I lift my nose into the air. "Oh, ye of little faith. You just wait. My Ursula is going to be both sexy and unique. I may not be a pro at romance or relationships, but I know how to Halloween."

"You use it as a verb," Violet says, arching a brow.

"I do." I narrow my eyes and smile. "And I think that tells you all you need to know about my dedication to celebrating this holiday properly."

"I stand corrected, then. And I can't wait to see the final result." She glances at her step tracker with a wince and a cluck of her tongue. "But if I'm going to be properly decked out myself, I've got to run. Marjorie can only squeeze me in for an up-do between five and five-thirty."

I make shooing motions. "Go. Get pretty. I'll see you at the party."

"Do I need to bring anything?" Violet asks, tossing her long hair over her shoulder as she backs toward the door. "Ice? Wine? Orange cupcakes with spider and skeleton rings on top?"

I shake my head. "Just bring yourself. According to Tristan, these people always hire a caterer, so…"

Violet rolls a shoulder. "Oh, well, oo-la-la. Hopefully my outfit will be up to snuff. I've never been to a fancy-person Healdsburg party before. My friends live over by the ball field and serve hot dogs. And they definitely want you to bring your own beer."

"He said they're super nice," I assure her. "And I'm sure your mystery costume will be fine. Seriously, you would look gorgeous in an old sack."

"But not in a gray wig," she teases, darting out of the bathroom before I can throw the bottle of shampoo at her.

"You'll see!" I shout. "It's going to be amazing."

"I bet it is," comes a deeper voice from down the hall, making my blood pressure spike. "Bye, Violet. Thanks for painting my sea witch."

"My pleasure. Your sea witch is looking pretty foxy in there in nothing but a bikini top, so be sure to brace yourself for impact," Violet says over the sound of the opening door. "See you two lovebirds later."

The door closes, leaving us alone, and when Tristan's voice comes again, I can tell he's even closer. "How did it turn out? I can't wait to see you."

"No! You can't come in here yet!" I grab the shower curtain, tugging it closed. "You can't see me until I'm all pulled together."

"But I want to see you now," he says from right outside the door. "A little bird told me you're only wearing a bikini top in there."

"And body paint you aren't allowed to smear until

after the party," I say in my I-mean-business voice. "I'm serious, Tristan, if you come in here before I'm ready I'm going to be for real angry with you. Proper Halloweening necessitates a big reveal."

"All right, all right. But I want to tell you something before I go shower, okay?"

I pull back the curtain. "Okay. What's wrong?"

"Nothing's wrong."

"You sound like something's wrong. Did you get another weird text from Kim?"

He hesitates for a long beat, making my stomach drop. I'd hoped Kim was getting the hint, but apparently not.

"Actually, she came by the shelter as I was closing up."

My forehead pinches. "What? Why? It's not like she can take an adopted animal back to Australia. They have very strict animal control laws down there."

"I know," he says, amusement in his voice before he continues in a more focused tone. "And no, she didn't want to adopt an animal. She said she was checking in to make sure I was okay. That I was safe..."

"Safe," I echo, frowning so hard I know I'm probably creasing my face paint. "From what? Surely she wasn't talking about like...safety in the bedroom, was she? Because that really is taking things *way* too far, even for her."

"Oh, she took things too far, but not like that. She told me a big story about how you stalked and victimized her in college. She even inferred that maybe your relationship with me is some elaborate plan to get back to terrorizing her. Or maybe a way to punish her for dating your ex."

My jaw drops. "What? Oh my God! That's such a load of...." I trail off, sputtering at the outrageousness of it all. "I mean, I don't even know what to call it. Bullshit is too tame a word. Horse shit, maybe? Rhinoceros shit? A giant floating whale turd? Whatever type of shit is the biggest and shittiest?"

Tristan chuckles. "Yeah, I figured. But since you haven't told me the real story, I didn't have much to fight back with, Zo."

I freeze, heartbeat slowing as I realize what Kim's done. She must have realized that I haven't told Tristan the truth about her sexploits in college for fear of hurting him. And now she's decided to use my good intentions to attempt to drive a wedge between Tristan and me.

I should tell him the truth—I know he'll believe my side of the story—but I just can't.

My reasons for holding my tongue still stand. Heck, they're standing even stronger than they did before. I don't just care about Tristan—I adore him. I'm crazy in love with this man, and my feelings only grow stronger with every passing day. I can't bear the thought of introducing pain into his life. Especially not because of a psycho ex-girlfriend who will be out of the country—and out of our lives—in a handful of weeks.

So instead of spilling the beans, I say, "I know. And I'm sorry about that, but I still think it's best to keep the past in the past. I can promise you that I never tried to hurt Kim in any way. That's just not who I am. But I really would prefer to leave it at that. Can you trust me? Even without all the gory details?"

"Of course I can," Tristan says without missing a beat. "And I do. You shouldn't be pressured into sharing things you're not ready to share because Kim is sticking her nose where it doesn't belong. I only want your secrets when you think I've earned them, Zoey."

Pain flashes through my chest. My first instinct is to swear to him that this has nothing to do with my secrets —that I'm only trying to protect him—but that would tip my hand and send him rushing to the very conclusions I'm trying to keep under lock and key. "Thank you," I say instead. "You really are the best."

"That remains to be seen. Let's see if I can coax Luke into his costume before we start handing out awesome boyfriend awards."

I grin. "No way. You're the awesome-est. Nominations are closed, and the envelope is sealed. And don't worry if Luke is skittish. I can wrestle him into his eel gear after I'm finished getting my costume on."

"Sounds good. I'm going to grab that shower. Can't wait to see the results of the transformation."

"Thirty minutes, maybe less," I promise as his footsteps move away down the hall.

I climb out of the tub, surveying my paint job in the bathroom mirror—Violet did a stellar job, and I can tell my face makeup is going to complement the pale purple base perfectly. My tentacle dress slides on easily over my swimsuit top and shorts, fitting even better than it did before, now that my padded bikini top is providing some extra stuffing up top, and my plastic shell jewelry provides the finishing touches. I apply my makeup—following the steps in a tutorial I found online—and finally slide the white wig into place, completing the look and standing back to soak in the big picture.

Even I, my own harshest Halloween critic, have to admit that I look incredible—sexy and a touch scary, with the combo of purple skin and black eyeliner making my eyes pop so bright and blue they look like they're glowing. The Sexy Ursula experiment is a complete success, but I can't seem to recapture the giddy excitement of earlier this afternoon, and I don't rush out of the bathroom to show Tristan the way I would have before he dropped the Kim bomb.

There's a bigger picture there, too, one I'm not seeing clearly, and that nags at my brain, dulling the innocent enjoyment of playing dress-up with the people I love.

Love...

I start to nibble at my bottom lip but force myself to stop before I smear my ruby red lipstick.

Kim still being in love with Tristan would explain why she's texting and swinging by the shelter to tell tall tales about how awful I was to her in college. Does she actually want him back? Or is this just her wanting to make sure he isn't happy with anyone else—or at least, not with me, the girl she decided to hate at first sight?

And where does Bear and the "patience" I heard them whispering about come in?

I feel like I'm right there, on the verge of pulling it all into focus... But before the puzzle pieces can fall into place, claws scratch against the door, and Luke lets out a mournful whimper.

"I'm coming, buddy, just a second," I say, giving my wig one last fluff. There will be time to sort out Kim's latest head game later. Tonight is for fun and friends and enjoying the spookiest night of the year with my amazing boyfriend.

I open the door to find Luke already dressed in his evil, green and purple, electric eel costume and Tristan standing behind him, looking a mind-melting mixture of ridiculous and sexy-as-hell that has me doubled over laughing in seconds.

Luke barks, bounding back and forth in the hall, clearly enjoying the excitement.

"This is not the reaction I was hoping for," Tristan says, running a hand down the front of his long white beard, the one that covers his chest but leaves his drool-worthy six-pack out for show-and-tell. "I'm a very serious merman, you know. I demand respect from my subjects, witch, not LOLs."

I stand, fighting to regain control and keep tears of laughter from slipping from my eyes and wrecking my makeup. "Oh, man, I'm so sorry, King Triton." I pat Luke on the head, helping to calm us both down. "You *are* very serious. I can tell by the lobster tucked in the front of your fins."

Tristan grins as he points at the stuffed lobster peeking out from the top of his sparkling blue merman tail—a pair of bellbottoms that flare into fins at his calves. "You like that? I ordered it on the sly to surprise you."

"Oh, I love it," I say, grinning so hard my jaw is starting to hurt. "Though I do feel tempted to ask if that's a lobster in your pants or if you're just happy to see me."

He moves in, wrapping his arm around my waist and drawing me close as Luke circles our legs. "Both, baby, because you are the sexiest sea witch in the ocean. How do you manage to look this hot painted purple?"

"Spring lilac, specifically. I tried on ten different colors until I found the perfect shade of sea witch."

"Oh, it's perfect, all right." His hand drops down to cup my ass above where one of my tentacles curls out into the air. "And the octopus look is really working for me. I think I'm developing a fish fetish as we speak."

"Octopi are mollusks, not fish." I arch an imperious brow even as I press closer, running my hands up his smooth, sculpted back, relishing the feel of his warm skin against my fingertips. "Cephalopods, in particular."

"I stand corrected, pet detective."

"Me, too," I say, smoothing his whiskers from his mouth. "I thought it would be easy to keep my hands off King Triton. I had no idea you would be this delicious. Ridiculous, but delicious."

"I had no doubt you'd be hot. You always are." His lids droop to half-mast, taking on that sexy, sleepy look that's growing more familiar with every passing day. It's an invitation I usually find impossible to refuse, but tonight—for the good of the trick-or-treaters of Healdsburg, who need to see our magnificent ensembles—I must fight the good fight.

"No way." I take a step back, moving out of his arms

and pointing a stern finger at his chest. "No pouncing until we party."

"Then I get to toss your tentacles over your head and take you like the king of the ocean?" he asks, sending a sizzle across my skin.

"Oh, yes," I promise, threading my fingers through his. "That sounds wonderful."

And it does—so wonderful I can't help skip-dancing through the house to the door, feeling like the luckiest girl in the world.

CHAPTER 20

TRISTAN

*O*utside, dusk has fallen, and a few tiny superheroes and toddler princesses are already making their way down the street from house to house—getting a jump on the trick-or-treating fun under watchful parental eyes before the big kids take over and run wild after dark.

Zoey and I leave our bowl of candy at the end of the drive by the smiling scarecrow she propped up on a throne of hay bales a few days ago, stick a sign saying *Take two, Happy Halloween!* into the nearly overflowing container, and head off with Luke trotting in front of us.

He's taken to his eel costume far better than I'd hoped, and it isn't long before he's drawing happy squeals of delight from trick-or-treaters. Zoey and I get our share of smiles, laughs, and compliments, as well. We're stopped twice for pictures on our way through the square—once by the Gazette photographer covering the annual festivities and once by a teenager wearing a terrifying clown costume, who swears that Ursula is her spirit animal.

By the time we reach the party on Johnson Street, things are already in full swing.

A song from *The Nightmare Before Christmas* blasts from the speakers, pumpkin lights hang in a crisscross pattern over the partiers in the walled-in backyard, and three older men dressed as Gandalf, Dumbledore, and the Wicked Witch of the West in drag are handing out candy to the early trick-or-treaters, clearly already a few beers into the twelve pack on the table behind their candy bin.

"Oh, my," Zoey says, pressing a hand to her lavender chest as her gaze sweeps back and forth across the lawn. "It's amazing! Like the Haunted Mansion at Disneyland, but a thousand times better."

"The Mortons don't play around when it comes to Halloween," I agree, admiring the cobwebs wafting from the trees in the front yard, the giant spiders crawling up the white siding of the old gingerbread Victorian, and the ghostly shapes moving in front of the darkened windows of the second floor.

There's an elaborate pet cemetery set up on one corner of the lawn, where motion activated black cats and ghostly dogs pop out from behind the gravestones as trick-or-treaters walk by. On the other side of the lawn is a gorgeous faux-marble statue of a Victorian woman whose eyes open and close every few moments —glowing red in the dusky light before winking shut again.

"And we haven't even made it to the backyard." I lean down to whisper in Zoey's ear, "That's where they have the haunted photo booth and the Morton kids' spooky tree house tour. They're teenagers now, so the tree house gets scarier every year."

"Wow. I'm blown away." Zoey reaches out to squeeze my hand as she lifts her sky-blue eyes to mine. "Thank you for bringing me. And for scoring an invite for Violet, too, so she won't have to spend the night alone. I can already tell this is going to be the best Halloween ever."

A rush of warmth floods through me, and it's all I can do not to kiss her sweet mouth and smear her sea witch lipstick. I adore this woman, every part of her— from the way she stands up for what she believes in, to her commitment to kindness in all things, to her devotion to excellence in Halloween costumes, and everything in between. "I wouldn't want to be here without you."

Truly, I don't want to be anywhere without Zoey, and I'm hoping she feels the same way. I'm taking a risk with the gift I tucked into the lobster puppet in my tail —she might think this is all too much, too soon—but I'm done second-guessing my gut or my heart. Especially when both are telling me to wrap this woman up in my arms and never let her go.

Bypassing the front porch, we head straight for the party-in-progress in the backyard. As we approach, a delighted squeal sounds from the gate. A moment later, it swings open and the Morton's oldest daughter, Grace, dressed as the Queen of Hearts from Alice in Wonderland, appears, waving us inside. "Get in here, you animals. Look at you three! You're fabulous! And purple makeup! That's so badass." She laughs a little too loudly, making me wonder how many cups of rum punch she's had already. "And I always knew Triton and Ursula were going to hook up eventually. I mean, I called that shit in sixth grade, didn't I, Mom?"

"Yes, Grace, but don't cuss in front of me, okay? Let me pretend college hasn't turned you into a hellion with the mouth of a sailor." Her mom, Deedee, grins at us and holds out two antique-looking goblets. "But she's right, you guys are absolutely fabulous. You might as well go straight over to the trophy table and grab first prize. Not a soul here will blame you. I'm Deedee, by the way. You must be Zoey. It's so nice to meet you."

"Nice to meet you, too." Zoey accepts her goblet and shakes Deedee's hand before Grace ushers us into the gazebo for the obligatory "arrival at the party" photo. The photographer urges us to look "fierce and fishy," and then the flash goes off, leaving us both blinking as we head to the refreshment table.

"They have a professional photographer, too?" Zoey whispers as I let Luke off his leash and he heads immediately for Clarence, the Mortons' basset hound, an old friend from the dog park who's camped out by the fire pit.

"They do, and they send out pictures via email after the party."

"ZOMG, that's amazing. I'll have a souvenir of how hot you are as a merman to pet and lick forever and ever." Zoey's eyes dance as she holds her goblet out for a fill-up from the mummy serving punch.

"You don't need a souvenir. I'll dress up as Triton for you anytime, baby."

Zoey wiggles her extra-dark Ursula brows at me as I wait for my serving of rum and fresh juice. "You're good to me, but Ursula is only out to play for tonight. Her makeup is way too high maintenance for a repeat performance any time soon."

"Understood," I say with a wink. "Guess I'll just have to make the most of my one night with the sea witch."

We wander away from the refreshment table and search the crowd chatting in chairs and comfy sofas on the large deck, waiting in line for a tree house tour, and dancing to "Witchy Woman" on the glowing dance floor.

"Do you see Violet?" Zoey asks, pressing up on tiptoe. "She said she was coming straight here from the hairdresser."

I scan the tops of the various female heads but don't see Violet's signature long, dark locks. "No, but she might be inside getting some food. They keep the full buffet in there to cut down on bug contamination."

"A full buffet." Zoey sighs happily. "Tell me they're serving shrimp that I can clutch dramatically between my blood-red sea witch nails, and I'll know that I've died and gone to heaven."

"I don't know, but we can go check."

"Yes, let's!" Zoey giggles as she grabs my hand, hauling me toward the back door. Inside, we move past another mini-dance-party—the under-ten set bobbing to something fresher than the old folks' tunes outside while throwing darts at a board on the wall—and into the massive kitchen. The buffet is laid out on the island, but the crowd is too thick to see from the door what's on offer, so Zoey and I slide into line behind an older woman dressed as a fairy godmother.

"Once we eat, I have something I want to show you," I say, unable to wait a minute longer to ask the question burning a hole inside me. "A secret passageway Deacon showed me when Tristan, Dylan, and I were kids."

"That would be amazing," Zoey says, bouncing on her toes. "Secret passageways are one of my top ten favorite things. Or they would be if I'd ever been through one before. And then can we go on the tree house tour? I'll have to get up there before I have more than one glass of punch, or I'm afraid I'll fall off the ladder."

"It has steps that wind around the tree," I say, taking a plate from the woman in a chef's coat manning a pan of dry-rub ribs. "So you'll be safe. Two please."

"Wow, they really do have all the bases covered. I'm so impressed." Zoey yips softly in excitement. "Oh, and Tristan look! Shrimp cocktail! Four o'clock! I've never been so glad I decided to be a pescatarian instead of a straight-up veggie girl."

I laugh, her excitement contagious. "Amazing. I'll get some, too. But we may have to put my lobster in the corner somewhere, so he can't witness the carnage. Because you know I'm going to have to take down a few of those crab legs, too."

Zoey nods soberly. "Some fish are friends; some are

food. This is something that Lobster is going to have to learn if he's going to be a part of this family."

Family...

It's the perfect word for what she, Luke, and I make together. And as we wind through the line, devour our dinner at a café table near the apple-bobbing station, and finally climb the stairs to the third floor of the old home, the last of my doubts about happily ever after fade away. The reason my first shot at forever failed was that Kim wasn't the person for me.

No, my capital O "One" was here under my nose all along.

Thank God I woke up and saw the writing on the wall before it was too late.

"Okay, this is the spot," I say as we reach the top of the stairs and step into the cozy reading nook on the landing, where there's just enough space for an over-stuffed chair, some bookshelves, and a small collection of jackalope-inspired art.

I pause, glancing over my shoulder to make sure no one's followed us.

I know the Mortons don't mind people who know about the secret passage bringing friends up, but they don't want everyone and their uncle wandering around on their roof, and they absolutely don't want kids up there unattended. "Keep watch while I pull the secret lever."

Zoey nods, fingers drumming on her goblet in antic-ipation. "This is so awesome," she whispers. "Where is the secret lever? And where is the door? It's behind the bookcase, right? Just like in an English manor murder mystery!"

Smiling at her over my shoulder, I nod. "It is. And the secret lever is hidden in plain sight…" I reach for the antlers of the largest jackalope, gripping tight as I turn the entire mounted head to the left, triggering the mechanism that unlocks the bookcase.

It puffs open with a rush of night air, and Zoey squeals softly in response. "Perfect! Perfect, perfect, perfect!"

Grinning, I open the bookcase-door wider and motion for her to take point. "After you, my lady."

Pausing to steal a quick kiss on her way by and whisper, "Perfect!" one more time, Zoey zips up the stairs in front of me, tentacles bobbing around her. After a deep breath and a silent prayer that this night ends the way I'm hoping it will, I follow her up onto the roof into the cool, starry night.

CHAPTER 21

ZOEY

From up on the roof deck, the night is even more magical. The view of the neighborhood's historic homes and the stars flickering in the velvety darkness make it feel like we're floating on a fairy ship through the night sky. The roughly twelve-foot area is octagonal, lined with benches on each of its eight sides and ringed with a wrought-iron railing featuring frog and princess designs that make the storytelling part of my brain run wild.

"Why princesses and frogs?" I run my fingertips over the curve of a frog's round cheek. "Were the original owners of the house hopeless romantics? Was he a frog she loved into a prince?"

"I'm not sure," Tristan says, "but their last name was Frogge, so that might have had something to do with it."

I turn to him with a wry smile. "Yeah? You think?"

"I think," he says, setting his glass on the bench

beside him with a rush of breath. "And I think there's something I should tell you, Zoey."

Sobering, I nod. "Okay. Is everything all right?"

He reaches for the lobster in his pants and tugs it out. "No, actually. There's something absolutely not right, but Lobster and I made a trip to the hardware store today to fix it."

Stomach dropping, I nevertheless force a breezy note into my voice as I set my own glass down. "So, the door's ready? I can move back to my place soon?"

Tristan shakes his head as he moves closer, wagging the lobster until something falls out into his palm, making me realize the crustacean is a puppet and the... whatever that is...was hidden inside. "No, the door's not ready, but this is." He holds the object up in the dim light. As my eyes adjust, I make out the shape of a small, gold key. "I don't want you to move out, Zo. I want you in my home, in my bed, in my life every second I can beg, borrow, or steal. I have never been happier than since you started sleeping over. I'm sorry it took me so long to realize how crazy I am about you, but I hope you'll consider taking this key so we can keep making up for lost time."

I blink faster. "You want me to move in with you? For real?"

"For real," he says. His vulnerable expression makes it clear he means every beautiful word he just said. "I also happen to be falling completely in love with you. I hope that's an acceptable part of the package?"

I cover my mouth with my hands as I nod, fighting happy tears.

"Is that a yes?" he asks.

"Yes," I whisper-sob. "Yes, you can fall in love with me. Because I'm already so desperately in love with you."

A smile breaks across his face as he reaches for me, sweeping me into his arms. "Thank God," he murmurs as he hugs me close.

I return the embrace, so happy I feel like laughing and crying at the same time. As Tristan wraps his arms even tighter around me, lifting me off my feet— smearing purple body makeup across his shoulders and giving me a mouthful of King Triton beard, in the process—I know I've found my perfect match.

He is the sweet, sincere, sexy, hard-working, hard-loving man of my dreams and all the proof I need that miracles can happen.

I'm floating on air, drunk on love and hope and all the glorious possibilities stretching out in front of us, and so giddy and filled with gratitude that the last thing I want to think about is Kim, Bear, or any of the ex-related drama.

But as Tristan and I pull apart, a flash of bright red on the street below catches my eye. When I turn my head—it's hard to ignore the bright blotch of crimson illuminated by the streetlight on the corner—I instantly recognize the woman dressed as sexy Red Riding Hood, complete with a long, flowing cape over a tiny pair of lederhosen.

The wolf she's arguing with is familiar, too. His back is to me, but I would recognize Bear's giant shoulders anywhere.

"Oh, man, don't look now," I grumble softly, nodding to the left. "It looks like we might have party crashers on our hands."

Tristan's brow furrows as his gaze shifts to the scene below. "Jesus... What is up with those two? I didn't even tell Kim we were coming to the Mortons. And she usually hates Halloween."

"I didn't tell Bear, either. He asked what we were up to tonight, but I was vague, and he said he and Kim were going to a party at the Raven."

Tristan turns back to me, nose wrinkling, making his beard shift higher on his face. "You talked to Bear? When?"

"This morning, he was hanging over the back fence again, pretending to pick oranges, and..." I trail off as my brain suddenly connects the dots. I look up at Tristan, eyes going wide as I pat his chest three times in rapid succession. "Oh my God, Tristan... They're faking it, too. They've been faking it from the start!"

He shakes his head. "What?"

"Bear and Kim!" I keep my voice low on the off chance my words might be heard on the street below. "They're not really a couple. They're pretending to be an item to make us jealous." I nod, chin bobbing as the pieces start coming together fast. "And I would bet my right hand that showing up at your brother's wedding reception wasn't a coincidence. They *planned* to be there, to shove their fake love in our faces while we were swept up in the romance of a wedding and use it to their advantage to make us start pining for them all over again."

Tristan curses beneath his breath. "I would say that's crazy, but..."

"But it's not crazy." I bite my lip as I probe my theory and find it holds water. "But they didn't plan on us pretending to be together, too. Our pretend threw their pretend off-balance, and they've been struggling to find their feet ever since. *That's* why Kim starting text-stalking you and Bear's been lurking in wait every morning when I take Luke out to the backyard. And then this morning, after Bear went back down the ladder, I heard Kim saying something about 'running out of time' and Bear telling her to be patient. I knew they were up to something, but I didn't want to say anything to you until I'd put the pieces together." I shake my head as I lift my spread fingers into the air at my sides. "Now it seems so obvious I can't believe I didn't figure it out sooner."

"Obvious that the people we were trying to fool were already fooling us?" he asks, arching a brow. "Seriously, don't be too hard on yourself. This entire thing is crazy."

"It is, right?" I say, laughter bubbling up inside me. "So, so crazy."

Tristan chuckles. "Seriously, it would be funny if they weren't both such complete pains in the ass."

"Well, to be fair, Kim is more of a pain in the ass than Bear," I say dryly. "I mean, at least he hasn't told any flaming lies in his attempt to come between us. He just drinks way too much fresh-squeezed orange juice and apparently loves chatting me up when I'm sporting PJs and an awesome case of bedhead."

"You're sexy in PJs and bedhead," Tristan says, wrapping his arms around me from behind as we both gaze down at the couple still conversing in harsh whispers on the street below. "I wonder what they're arguing about?"

"Hopefully Bear is refusing to crash the party," I murmur, "Kim is coming to terms with the fact that she's never going to win you back, and both of them will have left for Australia by tomorrow morning."

The words are barely out of my mouth when Kim whips her cell from the back pocket of her lederhosen and starts jabbing out a message as she paces the sidewalk in front of a clearly frustrated Bear. A moment later, my bottom buzzes.

I glance over my shoulder, brows lifted. "Is that a vibrating lobster? If so, color me intrigued."

Tristan grins wolfishly behind his beard. "Sadly, no. That's my cell tucked into the waistband of my boxer briefs."

I step back, watching him fish out his phone with amusement. "I could have brought a purse, you know. Carried your lobster and your phone for you."

"Please, woman. A real man carries his own lobster," he scoffs as he glances down at the screen. Immediately his grin fades. He lets out a tired sigh and turns the phone my way.

It's a text.

From Kim.

"Please listen, Tristan," I read aloud. "We need to meet. There's more to the story I started this afternoon.

I was afraid to tell you… I didn't want to hurt you… But now I know I can't wait any longer. I care too much about you to let you make a terrible mistake. I'm not backing down until we've talked for real, just you and me, someplace private where I can tell you everything."

I let out my own tired sigh and lift my gaze back to Tristan's face. "So much for coming to terms and going back to Australia. Are you just going to keep ignoring her?"

Tristan jabs the home button on his phone. "For now, but I've had enough of this. I need to figure out what I have to say to get her to leave us both alone."

"Maybe it isn't a matter of saying the right thing…" I press my lips together, gaze narrowing as Bear storms down the block away from the party and Kim—after stomping one red high heel on the ground and casting a resentful glare at the house—reluctantly follows. "Maybe it's a matter of *doing* the right thing. Actions speak louder than words, right?"

"What's going on in that head of yours?" Tristan asks, a smile in his voice. "Whatever it is, I want in."

I grin, rocking back on my heels as I rub my palms together, evil villain style. "Well, it would have to be something dramatic. A big, bold gesture…"

Tristan's eyes sparkle in the dim light reaching our perch from the lanterns below. "Big and bold. We pretend to elope?"

I clap my hands together, his words sparking inspiration. "Yes! But what if we take it a step farther?"

"I'm listening." He leans in, clearly intrigued.

"What about a fake wedding in our very own backyard? We could exchange vows close enough for them to hear every word from the other side of the fence."

"You really are brilliant." Tristan's hands circle my waist, squeezing lightly as he pulls me close. "And we'll get some friends and family to come and play along. Make it look like the real deal."

"And Violet can fake marry us." I skim my palms up to his shoulders. "She's an ordained minister."

"And Luke can be the flower dog," Tristan says, making my heart melt.

"Aw, he can. That'll be sweet." I cock my head, gazing up into Tristan's face. "So far our fake wedding sounds awesome."

"Totally," he agrees, bringing his face closer to mine. "And it'll be great practice, right? Just in case..."

"Just in case," I echo, my heart beating faster as the meaning of his words hits full force. He means, just in case we decide to get married for real...

"Too soon?" he asks, his breath warm on my lips.

"No," I murmur, heart singing. We just agreed to move in together. It should feel like too soon, but...it doesn't. And I'm too happy to pretend the thought of marrying Tristan would be anything but a dream come true. "No, it's not too soon," I add in a softer voice. "I want to spend as much time with you as I possibly can. Today and every day for the foreseeable future."

"Me, too," he says. "I love you, Zoey Childers."

"And I love—" His lips cover mine, cutting me off before I can finish.

But that's okay. He knows what I was going to say. It's clear in the way he kisses me, so sexy and sweet, each brush of his lips against mine a promise that we're going to keep making all our dreams come true. No matter what.

CHAPTER 22

TRISTAN

*I*t is a testimony to the awesomeness—and insanity—of my family that they met the news of my fake wedding to Zoey with general good cheer and threw themselves into making the occasion fun for all involved.

My brother Dylan offers to bring two kegs from his brewery, my brother Rafe and his wife, Carrie, insist on swinging by the farmer's market to get fresh flowers to decorate, and my sister-in-law Emma calls in a favor with a caterer friend to hook us up with a borrowed wood-fired pizza oven to roll into the backyard and a chef to whip up pizzas for the reception. My nephews assure Zoey and me that they've got DJ-ing under control, my older brother Deacon promises to make sure the boys throw in some old-folk friendly music along with their favorites, and offers up the tux he got married in years ago.

And for the finishing touch, Violet swings by late

Saturday night to squeeze in a fitting for Zoey, who will be wearing her old wedding dress.

"I'll have it hemmed and let out up top and ready to go by tomorrow morning," Violet promises, scooting through the living room with a garment bag under one arm and her sewing kit under the other. "I'm so excited! My daughters have already refused to wear my hideous old dress. I'm so happy it's going to get another turn down the aisle."

"It's not hideous!" Zoey insists, hurrying to open the front door for her. "It's gorgeous and elegant, and I'm so thankful. For the dress and the fake officiating and everything else."

Violet wrinkles her nose as she flaps a hand. "It's my pleasure. Anything I can do to help you two crazy kids get the crazier kids out of your hair."

Zoey and I wave goodbye and settle in for a movie on the couch with Luke snuggled between us, but it isn't long before we're both yawning.

"Planning a wedding—even a fake wedding—in less than forty-eight hours is exhausting," Zoey says, muffling another yawn.

"Agreed." I click off the television and stand, stretching my arms overhead. "So, did we decide to sleep in separate bedrooms tonight? To add realism to the fake wedding?"

Zoey huffs. "Heck, no. I plan on seeing you the night before the fake wedding, the morning of, and all of the days after."

I grin. "I like your style, soon to be fake Mrs. Hunter."

Her eyes twinkle. "I like the sound of that."

So do I…

* * *

I like it so much that by the next morning, as I take my place at the end of the aisle, waiting breathlessly for Zoey to step out the back door and onto the white canvas runner Violet brought with her, I know I'm not going to be able to hold out for long. One month, maybe two—the bare minimum to ensure Zoey takes my proposal seriously and my family doesn't insist we're both crazy—and I'm popping the question.

Though, I doubt my family is going to prove much of an obstacle to our happily ever after. It's clear they all love Zoey—from prickly, hard-to-impress Deacon, to the recently unjaded Rafe, to secretly soft-hearted Dylan and our even softer Pop, who I swear is going to bust a gut if Moo-donna doesn't give birth soon.

"I've got Sophie from the coffee shop on birth watch," Dad mumbles as he stands beside my brothers and me, looking dapper in his best blue suit. "She's going to text if anything happens while I'm gone."

"Sophie, huh?" I ask softly, keeping one eye on the door, not wanting to miss the moment Zoey steps through. "I didn't know you two were that close."

Dad clears his throat before adding a grumble, "Yeah, well…turns out there might be life after prostate cancer, after all."

I put an arm around his shoulders. "Good. I'm happy for you, Dad."

"And I'm happy for you, you pacifist nut job." He grunts. "If it were me, I would have clocked Zoey's ex in the face and told yours to stick her crazy where the sun don't shine, but..." He shrugs, his lips curving. "But this works, too. She's a sweet girl, your Zoey. Shame your mom's in Italy. I know she'd love to see you so happy, even if it is all a bunch of performance art."

"She would," Rafe agrees from Dad's other side. "And she would especially approve of the free pizza and beer."

"Hey, I paid for the beer," Dylan says from the end of the line, grinning at me. "But I'm happy to contribute. Zoey's a keeper, baby brother. And not just a pretend keeper."

"I know, I..." The rest of my words drift away, banished by a rush of excitement as the door opens and Luke trots out with a basket of flowers in his mouth, accompanied by Dylan's two-year-old daughter, Mercy, who toddles along beside the dog, throwing petals from the basket onto the ground.

A collective "aw" rises from the friends and family seated in simple white folding chairs on either side of the aisle, followed by a sigh as Zoey steps through the door, looking so stunning she takes my breath away. The dress is a simple cream off-the-shoulder number that falls in soft, flowing waves all the way to the grass. But the simplicity of the design only makes Zoey shine brighter. Her hair is piled on top of her head with pink roses tucked into her curls, her cheeks are flushed the same delicate pink as the petals, and her eyes are such a stunning, clear, sky blue I can't tear my gaze away from her.

As she walks slowly toward me, laughing as Mercy pauses to put some flower petals on Luke's head—seeming to think he could use some decoration, too—I see everything I've ever wanted, everything I'll ever need, right there in her eyes. In her sweet face, her kind heart, and her secretly wild and fearless spirit.

As she comes to stand beside me, the rest of the world fades away. I forget that my family is watching, I forget that this is a performance for our exes, who are very likely spying on us from the other side of the fence. I forget that this is all pretend and that when I go to bed tonight, Zoey won't truly be mine in the eyes of the law.

But that's okay.

She's already mine in all the ways that matter.

I take her hand, holding tight as we turn to Violet, feeling so emotional I'm not surprised that I struggle to get through the first few lines of the vows.

But by the time the rings are on our fingers and Violet invites us to speak a few words, I've found my center again.

I gaze down at Zoey and speak straight from the heart, "I used to think that love was a battle to be won, a struggle up a mountain that only the strong and persistent could survive." I pull in a breath, lips curving. "And then I kissed you, Zoey Childers. And from that moment on...everything was different. Thank you for showing me that love really can be patient and kind, and thank you for your patience with me, during all those months when I was too blind to see the truth right in front of my face. You are my truth, my love, my friend, and the best dog mom around. I don't know what Luke and I would do without you." Luke whines in what sounds like agreement, triggering a wave of soft laughter and a few sniffs from the assembled company. "I'm so honored for this opportunity to share my life with you."

Zoey swallows hard, blinking faster. "Wow. That's a tough act to follow. But I'll try." A smile trembles across her face as her grip tightens on my hands. "They say that the secret to everlasting love is falling for the same person again and again. Over the past few years, I tried to fall out of love with you so many times, Tristan Hunter. I was your employee and your friend and...I thought that's all we would ever be. But every time I was on the verge of getting my heart back under lock and key, you would do something wonderful or funny or kind, and it would go tumbling out of my chest again."

I brush my thumbs over the soft skin on the backs of her hands as I mouth, "Thank God."

She grins, her eyes shining brighter. "Deep down, I think I always knew that we would find our way to each other. But I'm so incredibly happy that the time is now. I'm so glad that I don't have to wait another day to start the rest of my life with you. I don't want to waste another day, another minute, away from you or Luke."

"Even though he's destroyed hundreds of dollars' worth of your socks and underwear?" Violet asks, making us all laugh and Zoey nod.

"Yes," she says, "even if I have to buy new socks every week for the rest of my life, it will be worth it. One hundred percent."

Violet hums in appreciation. "Amen. Then by the power vested in me by the Universal Life Church and by the state of California, I—"

"Stop! Wait! You can't marry her!" The shout comes from the other side of the fence, near the orange tree. A moment later, Kim's blond ponytail and panicked blue eyes appear over the top of the weathered brown boards.

A few shocked gasps sound from our friends and family and someone—I think my sister-in-law, Carrie—says, "You've got to be fucking kidding me." I glance from Kim to Zoey, whose wide eyes and dropped jaw leave no doubt she's as shocked by this development as I am.

Yes, we wanted to make sure Kim and Bear knew we were tying the knot, and we figured they'd get an eyeful of our Sunday morning celebration, but I never imagined that Kim would try to put a stop to the ceremony.

She's seriously lost her damned mind.

"Kim, please leave," I say firmly. "This is a private gathering."

"Tristan, please," she says, shaking her head frantically back and forth. "You don't have to do this. It's not too late to go back and make everything right. This isn't how this is supposed to end. You're supposed to be with me. We were made for each other. We've been in love since we were kids. Please, don't throw that away."

"I believe you're the one who threw my son away, Kimberly," Dad pipes up from behind me. "And I don't mind telling you that your grandmother would be ashamed of the way you treat people. Maggie was so sweet she wouldn't kill a cockroach in a corner, let alone sucker punch her own fiancé right in the heart."

"Dad, please," I begin, but before I can tell Dad I've got this, Dylan jumps in.

"You nearly broke him once, Kim," he seconds. "Why don't you crawl back to whatever hole you oozed out of and leave him the hell alone."

"That's enough," I say in a hard voice before Rafe or anyone else can add their two cents. "Thanks for the solidarity, but I don't need anyone to fight my battles for me." I glance back at Kim. "And there isn't any reason to be angry. I'm not. I'm grateful to you, Kim, I really am. If you hadn't left, I would have kept holding on so tight to tired old dreams I might never have seen that my one-in-a-million person was sitting next to me at the office every day." I tighten my grip on Zoey's hand and gaze down into her shining eyes. "I am so happy and so in love, and there is no doubt in my mind that this is where I belong. I thank God I found my way to Zoey." I shift my attention back to the fence. "And I thank you, too, Kim. So, thank you and goodbye."

Kim's bottom lip trembles as an incredulous look flickers across her features. "But she's lied to you, Tristan. She's tricked you. I didn't do any of those things that she said I did. I swear to you, I—"

"I haven't said anything about you, Kim." Zoey's words are soft but laced with steel. "I don't believe in hurting people for no reason, especially people I love."

Kim's jaw drops. "You're lying. I know you're—"

"No, she's not," a deep voice announces from the far side of the yard.

The heads of the gathered company swivel in unison as Bear strides swiftly around the side of the house still dressed in pajama pants and a gray T-shirt.

"I'm sorry for intruding, but I was afraid she was going to try something like this, and I wanted to be here to set the record straight." Bear motions to Zoey, regret creasing his features. "I'm sorry for interrupting your wedding, Zoey. And I'm sorry for sticking my nose back in your life when you clearly weren't interested in giving us a second chance. To express my sincere apologies, I'm here to shut this down, once and for all."

Zoey's lips part on a sharp inhale, but before she can speak, Bear barrels on.

"Kim cheated on you during college, bro." Bear shifts his attention my way with a wince, clearly taking no pleasure in delivering the news. "Zoey walked in on her with a couple of guys sophomore year, and Kim bullied her like crazy after. Like she blamed Zoey for—"

"He's lying," Kim screeches, her words ending in a sob.

"I'm not lying." Bear's brow furrows with determination. "And Kim and I aren't really a couple. We met up in Australia like I said, but we were both sad about leaving the people we loved behind, not interested in each other. We decided to pretend to be together to get you guys back, but obviously, that isn't working, so... I'm here to put a stop to it."

"I hate you, Bear," Kim shouts from the other side of the fence. "You're a fucking idiot. I never should have trusted you to keep your mouth shut." A moment later, the top of her blond head disappears, and the sound of angrily clicking heels on pavement fills the air as she storms away.

"You called it," I mutter to Zoey, who is looking up at me with eyes filled with concern.

"Are you okay?" she whispers, squeezing my fingers.

I blink, confused by the question for a moment until her meaning hits. "You mean about the cheating? Yeah. I'm okay. Truly." I smile. "It was sweet of you to try to protect me, but I don't need protection. And I don't care what happened in the past. I'm all about the future."

Zoey smiles. "Me, too."

"Then I guess I'll be going," Bear says from the far side of the lawn.

Still smiling, with her eyes firmly on mine, Zoey says, "Yes, please. Thank you, Bear. Have a good one."

"You're way too nice," Violet mutters before clearing her throat. "All right, then! If all the drama has reached its conclusion, I now pronounce, by the power vested in me by the—"

"The babies are coming!" my dad suddenly shouts, thrusting his phone into the air overhead as he grabs my arm. "They're coming, Tristan! We've got to go! Now!"

"What babies?" someone calls from the seating area. "Who's having a baby?"

"The cow's having twins," Deacon announces from the end of the line of Hunter men standing beside me, a hard eye-roll clear in his voice. "And I'm pretty sure she can do it without interrupting Tristan's wedding."

"Fake wedding," my dad huffs. "And you don't break

a promise for a fake wedding. Grab your toothbrush, Tristan, it might be a long night."

I cast a glance Zoey's way to find her laughing. "I'll pack a bag for you, grab us both a change of clothes, and meet you at the farm." She shoos her hands. "Go, help bring your grand cowbabies into the world."

"As long as everyone else stays and enjoys the pizza," I insist, allowing Dad to tug me away toward the back door. "And the beer."

"Got it covered," Dylan assures me. "We'll keep the oven warm for you until five, too, just in case."

But by the time five o'clock rolls around, Moo-donna is no closer to delivering, and even Sophie—who grew up on a dairy farm and insists twin births can be a long, drawn-out affair—is getting worried.

"I'll go wait in the driveway, bring the vet here as soon as she arrives," Zoey says, rubbing a comforting hand in circles on my back while I stroke Moo-donna's taut belly. She's definitely having contractions, but so far, they haven't progressed labor to the point we can see either of the calves, let alone get a calving rope around one of the baby's legs and help mama out.

"Thanks, babe." I wish I could hug her, but I'm already scrubbed to my elbows and have my heavy rubber gloves on, just in case. "Sorry about our fake wedding ending in a barn."

"Oh, please. It's fine. You know I'm more comfortable around animals, anyway. I just wish poor Moo-donna was having an easier time of it." She glances over her shoulder to where my dad is pacing back and forth on the far side of the barn, chatting urgently with Sophie. "And your dad, too. I've never seen him so stressed."

"Tell me about it," I mutter. "I think he's stressing out the cow. How is she supposed to relax with him hovering and muttering doom and gloom every five minutes?"

Zoey hums thoughtfully beneath her breath. "You could have something there. I'll see if I can get him to come wait with me. Give you guys a break in here."

"You're an angel," I say, adding in a softer voice. "And I'm really glad you took off your wedding dress to keep it clean, but will you promise to put it back on later? I was having fantasies about you in that dress and exactly how I was going to get you out of it."

Her eyes darken as she nods. "As long as you put on your tux, sexy. I can't wait to consummate the hell out of our fake marriage." She leans in, pressing a quick kiss to my lips.

Moo-donna groans a second later, her entire body shuddering beneath my hand.

"Got it. Sorry, Donna," Zoey says, pulling away. "I'm sure that isn't what you want to see right now, considering all the trouble kissing got you into."

"Do cows kiss?" I ask.

Zoey rolls her eyes. "Are you kidding? Of course, they do. Cows make out with their favorite friends for hours. They love kisses. And they adore being petted and have a keen memory for human faces, form strong bonds with their preferred cow buddies, and grieve deeply when they lose a member of their herd."

I nod soberly. "I think I just became a vegetarian."

"Good, I've got tons of recipes. You'll never miss meat, I promise." She winks as she slips out of the pen and closes the gate. "Be back in twenty minutes or less with the vet in tow."

But it turns out twenty minutes is about five minutes too late.

As soon as my dad is out of the barn—taking his stress vibes with him—Moo-donna gives a mighty push, and two spindly calf legs emerge into the cool evening air. A few pushes later, and I'm catching a gorgeous white and ginger-spotted calf in my arms. No sooner have I helped clear the fluid from his nostrils, than number two is on its way. Baby two is smaller, but the same beautiful cream and reddish-brown as his brother. It takes a little more work to get his nostrils clear, but just as I'm beginning to worry, the little guy coughs, sputters, and finally lets out a baby bellow for his mama.

Guiding the calves closer to Moo-donna—who immediately begins to give them both dozens of happy cow kiss-licks—I stand and strip off my gloves. I'm filthy and sweaty, and my back aches from crouching next to Moo-donna for hours, but those sweet little faces make it all worth it.

"Though, I have to confess I'm glad this wasn't the end of our real wedding day," I say to Zoey as we make our way back to her car an hour later—after a quick shower and a toast to the new additions with Sophie and Dad.

"Oh, I don't know," she says, looping her arm around my waist. "New life, new beginnings, helping an animal you love bring her first babies into the world... It seems like a pretty auspicious start to happily ever after to me."

I pause, turning to face her in the fading light, chest aching as I brush a loose curl behind her ear. "How do you do it?"

"Do what?" she asks, leaning her cheek into my hand with a smile.

"Make me fall deeper in love with you every day?" I ask softly, though I already know the answer. She doesn't have to do anything except be her sweet, sexy, thoughtful, completely adorable self.

She sighs happily and says, "Witchcraft," making me laugh.

"Witchcraft, huh?" I wrap my arms around her, pulling her close. "So are you a good witch or a bad witch?"

"I don't know," she says, a wicked grin curving her lips as her palms glide up my chest. "Why don't you take me home and find out?"

"In the car, woman," I say, my voice husky and my heart already beating faster. "I don't care what kind of witch you are, I want you in my bed ASAP."

"Take Eastside Road, it's fastest." She presses a breathless kiss to my lips before breaking away and jogging the rest of the way to the car.

Twenty minutes later, we're back at my place, discovering a note from Dylan assuring us that he and Tristan cleaned up the party mess and returned the pizza oven, the twins took Luke for a walk before feeding and kenneling him for the night, and Emma boxed up the leftover pizza and tucked it into the fridge in case Zoey and I were hungry.

And we are. We're starving, but that doesn't stop me from lifting Zoey onto the counter in the kitchen and kissing her senseless as she wraps her legs around my hips. It doesn't stop her from stripping my sweatshirt over my head or me from disposing of the sweater she changed into after the wedding.

We don't stop until her skirt is around her waist and her panties are on the floor, until my jeans and boxers are shoved down low enough to free my aching cock and I'm sliding inside her slick heat, thrusting deep into this woman who is my heart, my happiness, my future.

"I don't want to wait," I whisper against her lips as I rock inside her, loving the way her breath hitches as she clings to me. "Let's get married."

"Yes, oh yes," she says, as I grip her ass in my hands, pulling her closer at the end of each thrust, grinding against her clit.

"Yes to getting married or yes to me fucking you like this?"

"Both. Both, baby, yes, please," she says, kissing me with a soft laugh that becomes a gasp as I begin to drive deeper, harder, taking her with me to that bright, beautiful place I only find when I'm with her.

She comes a second before I do, her body locking tight around me, triggering a release so intense it nearly brings me to my knees. But it doesn't because Zoey is there, holding me tight, grounding me with her kiss, her touch, and her heart racing in time with mine.

Afterward, we start a fire, spread out a blanket for a dinner picnic, and make plans to elope over cold pizza and a bottle of Dry Creek Zinfandel. And though we realize some people might think we're crazy, we know the people who love us will understand.

Yes, Zoey and I are both usually cautious people, but when something's right, it's right, and there's no doubt in either of our minds that this is where we want to be. Whether we take a year to plan a big wedding or run away to Vegas next weekend, the end result will be the same—Zoey and me, together, looking forward to all the dreams we're going to make come true as husband and wife.

"You're sure you won't miss the dress and the flowers and all that?" I ask as I finish off the last slice of feta and rosemary pizza.

"I've already had the dress and the flowers," she says. "And we've already had all the people we love there while we said our vows. As far as I'm concerned all that's missing is the paperwork."

"And a honeymoon." I bob my eyebrows suggestively. "A long honeymoon."

She grins. "I think four days is all we can get away with on such short notice, but we could always call this the practice honeymoon and take a longer trip over the Christmas holidays."

"I like the way you think," I say, leaning in for a kiss.

"And I like the way you make love to me in the shower," she murmurs against my lips. "Which reminds me... I'm feeling kind of dirty after all that time in the barn."

"Well, I like you dirty, but I'll most happily help you get clean, soon-to-be Mrs. Hunter." I stand, helping her to her feet before sweeping her into my arms and making a beeline for our bedroom.

Ours, where I hope to get clean and dirty and everything in between with this woman for many years to come.

EPILOGUE

LUKE

Two years later...

My humans are the best humans—truly wonderful two-legs in every way.

I've known they were special from the moment I met them, but they've really outdone themselves with the new puppy.

The new puppy is beautiful.

The new puppy is a chubby little angel with the softest cheeks and the best giggle I've ever heard.

The new puppy also occasionally squeezes my ears too tight, but I understand—puppies don't know any better, and a pinched ear is a small price to pay for the sweetest treat on the face of the great green earth.

Puppy socks...

The sight of them lying there on the quilt as Zoey changes the puppy's diaper—two tiny scraps of blue, fresh from the puppy's sweet, sweaty little feet—is enough to make my mouth water. I wipe my muzzle on my front legs, trying to hide my excitement as I inch closer to my prize on my belly, waiting for the perfect moment.

"Don't even think about it, Luke," Zoey says, her back still turned to me. "Those socks are going in the washing machine and nowhere else."

I whine softly, making Tristan laugh as he emerges from the hallway dressed in baggy clothes with straw sticking out of the arms and legs. "She's got eyes in the back of her head, man. You should know that by now." He crouches down beside Zoey, depositing a heap of brown fabric onto the quilt. "One cowardly lion costume, Dorothy. Should I get the Tin Man into his gear or wait until you've got Gabe ready to go?"

"Go ahead and dress Luke," Zoey says. "Gabe is clean and changed, and we'll be ready to go in a few minutes. Right, buddy?" She squeezes the puppy's tiny feet. "Are you excited for your first Halloween?"

The puppy burbles happily, waving his chubby fists in the air as Tristan and Zoey beam down at him with love in their eyes.

"I'm excited, too," Tristan says, rubbing a hand up and down Zoey's back. "I love you guys."

"And we love you, too, baby." Zoey turns to Tristan, smiling as she brings a hand to his cheek. They both get that look in their eyes—that soft, melting, grateful look that means they're about to kiss—and I brace myself.

This is my one shot…

My last chance…

My final opportunity to score those sweet, sweet socks for my very own...

I hold my breath, watching as my two favorite humans move together, their lips meeting in a way that leaves no doubt how much they love each other. I wait until their eyes slide closed and then—I pounce!

Quick as a flash, I'm on the quilt, snapping the tiny socks into my mouth, and bolting for the basement. By the time Zoey shouts—"Bad dog, Luke! Bring those back!"—I'm already down the stairs, bounding into the corner behind my kennel, where I lie down to relish the exquisite flavor of puppy feet.

I taste salt and milk, sweat and puppy funk, and an earthy undertone that reminds me of long days running through the grass and hot summer rain. I close my eyes, soaking the sweet taste into my soul for a few precious moments before Tristan appears on the other side of my kennel.

"Are you going to drop them on your own, or do we have to wrestle?" he asks, propping his hands on his hips. "Come on, buddy. Drop the socks. You don't want to end up at the vet tonight, do you?"

Of course, I don't—and I haven't *eaten* a sock since long before the puppy was born, I've just *tasted* them.

It would be nice to get a little credit for my self-restraint, but I can't blame Tristan and Zoey for hoarding the socks for themselves. It is *their* puppy, after all, and after all the work they do to keep the little guy fed and clean and happy, they ought to be able to enjoy a chew on his socks at the end of a long day.

Exercising the maturity I've worked hard to develop

since becoming a big brother, I pad around the kennel and drop the now soggy socks at Tristan's feet.

"Good boy," he says, scratching my neck the way I like, getting deep under my collar. "Now let's get you dressed. It's almost party time."

Back upstairs, Tristan helps me into a silver costume with a generally irritating cone hat I intend to rub off at the first opportunity, while Zoey dresses our puppy, who is even cuter with his cherub's face ringed with a lion's mane.

Not long after, we're out in the cool autumn air, Zoey pushing the stroller as we head to the annual spooky gathering, where I will steal all the treats the little humans and the humans who've had too much wine drop on the grass, run and play with my friend Clarence, and dance with Tristan, Zoey, and our puppy.

My humans are excellent dancers.

And excellent people.

And excellent parents.

I truly can't imagine a better pack to be a part of than this one. Though, if Tristan and Zoey decide to have more puppies, that would be nice. We've got more than enough love in our house to go around. More puppies would just mean more love, more happiness, and of course...more socks.

The thought makes me smile as we reach the party and head for the gate.

It's a sweet life, all right.

Sweet and getting sweeter every day.

The End

TELL LILI YOUR FAVORITE PART

I love reading your thoughts about the books and your review matters. Reviews help readers find new-to-them authors to enjoy. So if you could take a moment to leave a review letting me know your favorite part of the story —nothing fancy required, even a sentence or two would be wonderful—I would be deeply grateful.

Thank you and happy reading!

SNEAK PEEK

The NHL's biggest bad boy is about to fall for the virgin next door...

I am the world's biggest dating failure. We're talking my last date went home with our waitress kind of failure.

But I have an ace in the back pocket of my mom jeans— my sexy-as-sin best friend, NHL superstar forward, Justin Cruise.

Justin owes me favors dating back to seventh grade, long before he became a hotshot with a world famous... stick. So in return for my undying platonic loyalty, all I want is an easy-peasy crash course on how to be a sex goddess.

How hard can it be?

* * *

I have never been so hard in my life.

The things I want to do to my sweet, kindergarten-teaching, mitten-crocheting best friend Libby Collins are ten different kinds of wrong. Maybe twenty.

But I'm a firm believer in teaching by example, and by the end of our first lesson, we've graduated to a *hands on* approach to her sexual education: my hands all over her, her hands all over me, and her hot mouth melting beneath mine as I prove to her there isn't a damned thing wrong with the way she kisses.

Give me a month, and I'll transform Libby from wall flower to wall banger, and ensure she's confident enough to seduce any guy she wants.

Problem is… the only guy I want her seducing is me.

Hot as Puck is a sexy, flirty, friends-to-lovers Stand-alone romantic comedy from *USA Today* Bestseller Lili Valente.

Please enjoy this excerpt from
HOT AS PUCK!

Justin

This is it, the night I'll look back on in fifty or sixty

years and stab a finger at as the moment my life changed forever. Somewhere out there, in the throng of people wiggling to the club beat pulsing across the Portland skyline from the most exclusive rooftop lounge in the city, is the woman I'm going to marry.

Next summer.

In eight short months.

Because I'm dying to settle down, develop a food-baby where my six-pack used to be, spend Friday nights on the couch in my give-up-on-life sweatpants arguing about what to watch on Netflix and picking out names for the five or six kids my wife and I will bang out as quickly as possible to ensure we'll have an army of small people to share in the grinding monotony of our wedded bliss.

Ha. Right.

Or rather *no*. Hell no. Fuck no, with a side of "what kind of reality-altering drugs have you been huffing in the bathroom?"

Sylvia is out of her goddamned mind! I'm twenty-eight years old—tonight, happy fucking birthday to me —and at the top of my game. I have zero interest in a long-term commitment to anything but my team.

The Portland Badgers are riding a ten-game winning streak, thanks largely to the fact that I bust my ass in the gym every other morning so I can bust my ass on the ice every time Nowicki spaces-out eighteen minutes into the period and forgets what his stick is for. That rookie's untreated ADHD is a pain in my ass, but the rest of the forwards and I are taking up the slack and then some. I'm averaging over a point a game, leading the league in goals, and on my way to an elite season. Maybe even an Art Ross Trophy-winning season, though I don't like to count my eggs before they've been scrambled, smothered in cheese and hot sauce, and wrapped in a burrito.

God, a burrito sounds good. I'm so fucking hungry. I would kill for Mexican right now, or at least something cooked and wrapped in something other than seaweed.

Nearly three thousand dollars in hor d'oeuvres are being passed around this party on shiny silver platters, and there's not a damned thing I want to eat.

I let Sylvia—who has very firm opinions about many, many things—handle ordering the food, and apparently she thought sushi, sushi, more sushi, and some weird, rock-hard, low-fat cookies that taste like vanilla-flavored air were all anyone would want to shove in their pie-hole tonight. Just like she thought I should get down on one knee and put a ring on her finger in time to plan a blockbuster summer wedding or she would need to "explore her other options."

Explore her other fucking options. What the fuck? Who says something like that to a guy they swear they're desperately in love with? If she were really that gone on me, wouldn't I be the *only* option? The only person in the entire world that she could even remotely consider spending the rest of her life with?

I kind of want to hate Sylvia—what sort of person tries to blackmail you into proposing to them on *your* birthday? She should have at least waited until *her* birthday next month—but I just keep thinking about how lonely my bed is going to be tonight. Sylvia is clearly deeply deluded about how far along we are in the evolution of our relationship, but she's also very pretty, gives the best head I've ever had, bar none, and smells really, really nice.

I have a thing about the way a woman smells. Not her perfume or her soap or her body lotion, but *her*. The woman herself. Her base note, the scent that rises from her skin when she's lying in the sun or kissing me after a run or just hasn't showered in a while.

Yes, with the right woman, I enjoy logging some quality bedroom time while she's a little bit dirty. Don't fucking judge me! It's my birthday!

Anyway... No one smells as good as Sylvia does at the end of a long day on my boat, with sweat, sea salt, and sunscreen dried on her skin. Making love to her on the deck this past summer, with her long legs wrapped around my waist as I did my best to take home the trophy for most orgasms delivered in a single afternoon, I was convinced I'd finally met someone I could stick with for longer than a season.

But it's not going to happen. It's only October and I've just told Sylvia she's coo-coo for Cocoa Puffs and that I'll have her shit packed up and sent to her office tomorrow afternoon.

And then she said that I was an emotionally unavailable jerk who is incapable of sustaining an adult relationship. And then I said that she's a blackmailing, birthday-ruining, manipulative, sushi-obsessed control freak who should try to choke down a carb once in a while because it might make her more fun to be around on pizza night or donut morning or any other day of the goddamned week involving carbs because a life without carbs is a stupid life. And then she flipped me off and told me to "have a nice long, lonely existence, asshole," before knocking over a tray of champagne glasses on her way to the elevator at the other end of the roof.

The only good news? Very few of my guests seemed to notice our fight or Sylvia's dramatic exit.

It's nine-thirty, we've all been drinking since six, and most of my nearest and dearest are feeling no pain. I should be feeling no pain, too. I'm on my third tumbler of GlenDronach, haven't eaten anything since lunch because the food at my party is unacceptable—if Sylvia and I were really meant to be, she would have realized I hated sushi two months ago—and haven't drunk anything more serious than a beer since before the preseason.

But somehow, I'm stone-cold sober.

Sober and tired of celebrating, and wishing I could slip out and grab a deep-dish pizza from Dove Vivi. The cornmeal crust thing they've done to their pies is addictive, and I'm pretty sure there's nothing in the world fresh mozzarella, house-made bacon, and a hearty slathering of pesto can't fix.

Portland is home to some of the best eats in the world. It's also home to more strip clubs per capita than any other city in the nation. If I weren't committed to being a good host, I could have pizza in my belly and boobs in my face in under an hour. But I'm not the kind to ghost on my guests. I leave that for weirdos like my team captain, Brendan, who consistently vanishes from bars and clubs without warning, and clearly has issues with saying good-bye.

Not that I can blame him. After six years as a happily married man, going back to hitting the scene solo can't be easy.

I'm just glad to see him finally out and about again. After Maryanne's death, he shut down so hard a lot of us on the team were worried there might come a day when we'd show up for practice and learn Brendan wasn't coming back to the ice, either because he'd lost the will to play, or because he'd lost the will to live.

That's how much you should love the woman you're going to marry. You should love her so much that if she were taken away from you it would feel like your rib cage had been cracked open and some sadistic son of a bitch was cutting away tiny pieces of your heart, slathering them in salt, and eating them right in front of you.

I've never felt anything close to that. For Sylvia or any other girl I've dated.

So maybe Sylvia is right. Maybe I'm going to spend the rest of my life solo, with my loneliness occasionally broken by short-term relationships with various hot pieces of ass.

"Poor me," I say, lips curving in a hard grin.

Seriously, cry me a river, right? I've got a multi-million-dollar contract, a stunning loft with one-hundred and eighty degree views of the city, and my health, which is not something I'm stupid enough to take for granted. I was born with the kind of face that not even a black eye from scrumming with those douchebags from L.A. can wreck, and a body that performs—on the ice and in the bedroom. I should be laughing all the way to the dance floor, where I know of at least six or seven unattached hotties, any one of which would be happy to ease my birthday breakup pain by riding my cock all night long.

What do I want instead?

Pizza. My pajamas. And a crochet hook with an endless supply of yarn.

Nothing calms me down like hooking on a granny square until I've got one big enough to cover my entire damned bed. I've graduated to more complex projects since those early days learning how to hook so I wouldn't go crazy while I was stuck in bed with mono for three months, but sometimes mindless repetition is the only cure for what ails me.

And yes, I like to crochet. Again, I'll ask that you not fucking judge me, because it's my birthday, because my charity, Hookers for the Homeless, has provided over two thousand caps, gloves, and scarves to people in need, and because my Instagram account—Hockey Hooker—has over a million followers. Clearly, the women of the world have no problem with a man who enjoys handicrafts. Though, the fact that my first post was a body shot of me wearing nothing but a Santa Hat I'd crocheted over my cock probably didn't hurt.

I have no shame when it comes to selfies with my latest project. My friend Laura—childhood partner in crime and current public relations master for the Badgers—says she approves of my social media efforts to promote good will for the team. Her little sister and my crochet guru, Libby, thinks it's great that I'm using my yarn addiction to raise awareness of the homeless crisis. But let's get real. I started posing semi-nude for the tail and the attention.

I'm usually a big fan of tail and attention.

But now, as Laura and Libby climb the steps leading up to the patio from the dance floor, clearly intending to wish me a warm, bubbly, old-friends happy birthday, I wish I had an excuse not to talk to either one of them. Laura because she's insane when she's drunk—once she's had a few, the usually level-headed La can't be trusted not to embarrass herself and everyone around her—and Libs because I'm incapable of hiding anything from that girl.

Ever since thirteen-year-old Libs spent months teaching me how to crochet when I was housebound my sophomore year of high school—keeping me company and furthering my yarn-based education while we watched 80s movies and debated important things like whether *Better Off Dead* or *Just One of the Guys* was the superior underrated teen flick of that particular decade—I've had a chink in my armor where the youngest Collins sibling is concerned.

She sees through me. Every damned time.

When I had a shitty first half of my first season with the Badgers five years ago, Libby was the one who noticed I was being eaten alive by self-doubt and talked me back from the edge. When my charity was getting audited by the IRS, Libby realized I wasn't nearly as chill about the whole thing as I was pretending to be and sent me a knight's helmet she'd crocheted and a note promising that everything would work out. And when Sylvia and I had a pregnancy scare last summer, Libby was the only person I told.

Hearing Libs say that I could absolutely handle being a dad had made me a little less terrified. Not that I'd believed her, but hearing that trying your best and loving your kid is all that really matters from a woman who spends every day with a classroom full of rug-rats was comforting.

But I don't want to be comforted right now. I want to get through the rest of this party and then hide out at home and lick my breakup wounds in private. So I plaster on a smile and hope it's too dark for Libby to see how shitty I feel.

"Hello, birthday boy!" Laura throws her long arms around me, hugging me hard enough to make my breath rush out with an *oof* as she crushes my ribs, reminding me she's also freakishly strong when she's three sheets to the wind. "I love you, Justin. I'm so glad we're still best friends. Let's go do happy-birthday shots on the roof to celebrate!"

"We're already on the roof." I grunt again as she hugs me even tighter.

"Yes, we are, and as high up as anyone needs to be right now," Libby agrees, meeting my pained gaze over her sister's shoulder, her brown eyes anxious. Clearly, she's also aware that her big sis has entered the bad-decision-making portion of the evening and should be monitored closely until she's home in bed.

"No, the real roof, the one through the locked door behind the DJ booth." Laura points a wobbly hand toward the stairwell on the other side of the dance floor, then twists her long red hair into a knot on top of her head. "I've been practicing my lock-picking skills so I'll be ready when I quit PR to become a spy."

"As one does," I observe dryly.

"Exactly!" Laura jabs a bony finger into the center of my chest. "See, you get it. So let's do this. We'll break the lock, climb the stairs, and be the highest things in downtown. Get shots and meet me there. Or maybe we should stick with martinis." She moans happily as she wiggles her fingers in the general direction of the bar. "Those Thai basil martinis are so amazing! Perfect with the sushi. Like, seriously brilliant. Sylvia did a bang-up job with the catering, Jus. Especially for a woman who looks like she hasn't eaten since last Christmas."

"Laura, hush," Libby whispers, nudging her sister in the ribs with her elbow.

Laura bares her teeth in an "oh shit" grimace before smacking herself on the forehead. "Fuck, I'm sorry. I forgot about the storming out and knocking over a tray of drinks on her way out of the party thing. Are you two okay?"

"We're fine," I say, cursing silently. So much for avoiding this particular conversation. "She just decided it wasn't working for her. It's no big deal."

"But breaking up on your birthday sucks." Laura's lips turn down hard at the edges. "And I thought she was one of the nice ones. I mean, I didn't know her that well, but she seemed nice."

"She was nice." I take another too big drink of my scotch. "And now she's gone. But she hadn't even unpacked her boxes yet, so it shouldn't take long to move them all out."

"That's right. I forgot you two had moved in together. Bet that makes you want to keep drinking, huh?" Laura reaches back, putting an arm around Libby, hugging her much shorter sister closer as she not-so-subtly tries to steal Libby's martini.

Libby, who I suddenly realize is looking very un-Libby-like in a tight black tank top and a pair of leather pants that cling to her curvy thighs, huffs and swats Laura's hand away. "Enough! Stop using displays of affection to try to steal my drink."

"Why? It worked last time," Laura says, grinning wickedly.

"Well, it's not going to work this time. I'm keeping my martini." Libby narrows her eyes, which are ringed in heavy black liner and some silver glittery stuff that emphasizes how enormous they are. It's a look that's way more rock-star than kindergarten teacher and also decidedly...odd. For her, anyway.

I can't remember the last time I saw Libby wearing makeup or tight clothing. She's a "layers of linen draped around her until she looks like an adorable bag lady or a hippie pirate" kind of girl. I'm used to the Libby who wears ruffly dresses, clogs, and crocheted sweaters, and totes her knitting bag with her everywhere she goes.

This new look is so unexpected that I'm distracted long enough for Laura to snatch my scotch right out of my hand.

"Hey, give that back," I say, scowling as she dances

out of reach. "It's an open bar, psycho. Go get your own scotch."

"But it's more fun to steal yours," Laura says. And then, with the gleeful giggle of a woman who is going to be very hungover tomorrow morning, she turns and flees into the throng of dancers writhing to the music, tossing, "Come get me when it's time to break and enter! You know you want to," over her shoulder.

Libby sighs heavily, and I turn back to see her watching me with that same anxious expression, making my heart lurch. "I don't want to talk about Sylvia," I say, cutting her off before she can ask.

"Okay," she says, letting me off the hook far more easily than I expect her to. "But can we talk about something else? Something kind of...private?"

"Um, sure." I do a quick scan of our immediate surroundings. Aside from a couple making out in the shadows about ten feet away, we're alone. Everyone else is either out on the dance floor, queued up at the bar, or lounging on the couches near the fire pit on the other side of the patio, soaking in the view of the city.

"Thanks." Libby smiles nervously as she lifts her glass. "Just let me down a little more liquid courage first."

"All right," I say, wondering who this woman is and what she's done with my sweet, rarely drinks more than one drink, doesn't own a stitch of black clothing, would never leave the house without putting on a bra Libby.

I really don't think she's wearing a bra under that lacy shirt. And I really can't stop staring, trying to solve the bra or no-bra mystery, and I'm swiftly becoming way too fixated on Libby's breasts for my personal comfort.

"Maybe I should get a drink, too." I start for the bar, needing a moment to pull myself together, when Libby puts a hand on my arm.

"I'm sorry," she says, but I have no idea what she's apologizing for, only that her touch feels different than it did before. As different as the Libby I've known since she was a kid is from this seriously sexy woman standing in front of me.

HOT AS PUCK is Available Now!
Learn more at Lili's website.

ABOUT THE AUTHOR

USA Today Bestselling author Lili Valente has slept under the stars in Greece, eaten dinner at midnight with French men who couldn't be trusted to keep their mouths on their food, and walked alone through Munich's red light district after dark and lived to tell the tale.

Find Lili on the web at
www.lilivalente.com

The Master Me Series,
red HOT erotic Standalone novellas!
SNOWBOUND WITH THE BILLIONAIRE
SNOWED IN WITH THE BOSS
MASQUERADE WITH THE MASTER

Bought by the Billionaire Series—
HOT novellas, must be read in order.
DARK DOMINATION
DEEP DOMINATION
DESPERATE DOMINATION
DIVINE DOMINATION

Kidnapped by the Billionaire Series—
HOT novellas, must be read in order.
FILTHY WICKED LOVE
CRAZY BEAUTIFUL LOVE
ONE MORE SHAMELESS NIGHT

Under His Command Series—
HOT novellas, must be read in order.
CONTROLLING HER PLEASURE
COMMANDING HER TRUST
CLAIMING HER HEART
Under His Command Trilogy-*USA Today* Bestseller

To the Bone Series—

Sexy Romantic Suspense, must be read in order.

A LOVE SO DANGEROUS

A LOVE SO DEADLY

A LOVE SO DEEP

Fight for You Series—

Emotional New Adult Romantic Suspense.

Read in order.

RUN WITH ME

FIGHT FOR YOU

Bedding The Bad Boy Series—must be read in order.

THE BAD BOY'S TEMPTATION

THE BAD BOY'S SEDUCTION

THE BAD BOY'S REDEMPTION

The Lonesome Point Series—

Sexy Cowboys written with Jessie Evans.

LEATHER AND LACE

SADDLES AND SIN

DIAMONDS AND DUST

12 DATES OF CHRISTMAS

GLITTER AND GRIT

SUNNY WITH A CHANCE OF TRUE LOVE

CHAPS AND CHANCE

ROPES AND REVENGE

8 SECOND ANGEL

Made in the USA
Middletown, DE
30 August 2021